PRIMED FOR
THE STEELE TEAM

"You and me, police man," Ice said. "That's the deal. *Cooperation*. Anything you get, I want a piece of. All except for Victor Borodini. I want *that* man all to myself."

"You're not in any position to make demands, Ice," Steele said. "If Higgins wanted to, he could open you up like a tin can. Give you a little shot and you'd tell him everything you know with a great big stupid smile on your face. In fact, I wonder why he didn't do that."

"I'll *tell* you why, police man. Because it ain't what I know so much as *who* I know and who I can *get* to," Ice said. "They need me to get 'em. And I need you to balance off Borodini's muscle. We need each other, Steele. You scratch my back, I scratch yours."

"If I wanted a partner," Steele said, "you'd be the *last* one that I'd pick. I work alone."

STEELE!

The perfect combination of man and machine—the ultimate cop!

COLD STEELE

J. D. MASTERS

CHARTER BOOKS, NEW YORK

COLD STEELE

A Charter Book/published by arrangement with
the author

PRINTING HISTORY
Charter edition/November 1989

ISBN: 1-55773-278-7

Charter Books are published by The Berkley Publishing Group,
200 Madison Avenue, New York, New York 10016.
The name ''Charter'' and the ''C'' logo are trademarks
belonging to Charter Communications, Inc.

PRINTED IN THE UNITED STATES OF AMERICA

10 9 8 7 6 5 4 3 2 1

For Jim Morris,
who saw the possibilities,
with special thanks to J. Kennedy and Kevin Bishop

1

The army chopper came in low over the East River and landed on the helipad just below FDR Drive, about a mile south of the ruins of the 59th St. Bridge. Dev Cooper picked up his bag and stepped out through the hatch, ducking low to avoid the rotating blades. A car waited for him. The driver was a uniformed marine sergeant in full dress blues. He wore a 9 mm. semiautomatic on his belt in a white flap holster.

"Dr. Cooper?" he said, approaching and snapping off a sharp salute. "Welcome to New York, sir."

A civilian, Cooper did not know if he was expected to return the salute or not, and he would have felt awkward doing so in any case. Instead, he merely nodded and touched the brim of his chocolate-colored Stetson. The marine dropped his salute.

"Hope you had a nice flight from New Mexico, sir," the marine said. "My name is Sgt. Coles. May I take your bag?"

"Thank you, Sergeant," Cooper said in soft western drawl, relinquishing the suitcase.

"Is that all you brought, sir?"

"Yes, I like to travel light."

"Best way to do it," Coles said, walking him back to the car. He opened the trunk and put the suitcase in, then opened the rear door of the limo for him. "If you'd care for a drink to freshen up, sir, there's Scotch, bourbon, vodka, rye, and Tennessee sour mash in the bar. You'll find ice in the compartment to the right, next to the glasses."

1

"Appreciate it," Cooper said. "A shot of bourbon would hit the spot. How far do we have to go?"

"It's only a short drive to the Federal Building, sir. We'll be there in a couple of minutes. In fact, you can see it right over there."

He pointed to the tall glass slab rising over the East River, the building that had once housed the United Nations headquarters.

Cooper glanced briefly at the skyline of Manhattan. From the ground, it looked even more inhospitable than it had appeared from the air. The concrete towers were a far cry from the red adobe buildings of Santa Fe. Just looking at it made him feel claustrophobic. He had never been to New York before. He had been to Phoenix once, and that city had struck him as looking far too dense and sterile. This was even worse. And now he'd have to make his home here.

As the limo cruised along FDR Drive, he sipped his bourbon and wondered for about the dozenth time since he left Santa Fe what he was letting himself in for. Only a few days ago, he had been working on a federally-funded project at Los Alamos dealing with psychocybernetics, a branch of science he had not been trained in, but which represented a unique opportunity for psychological research. He was trained as a psychiatrist, specializing in abnormal psychology and stress-related conditions. The Los Alamos project, a branch of a government-sponsored study known as Project Download, had been concerned with the study of brain/computer interface, and he had been brought in to study the human aspect of the problem.

The working conditions were, to say the least, a bit unusual. Most of his colleagues on the research staff were cybernetics engineers, which made for some interesting conversations over lunch in the project cafeteria and at dinner parties after work. As a group, engineers were not much given to abstract thinking, though cybernetics engineers were a bit more freewheeling and progressive in their attitudes. Most of them were fairly young, and they had a tendency to dress very casually in jeans, open-necked shirts and sneakers.

Many of the men wore their hair long and had beards; the women generally wore jeans and boots or denim skirts, plaid shirts and sandals. Nobody ever wore a tie. His silver bolo was the only sort of neckwear in evidence. The atmosphere was less that of a government-sponsored project than a university lab.

At first, he had felt very out of place. At forty-two, he was at least ten years older than most of the other project staff, and he didn't understand 90% of what they were talking about. They had their own lingo, which sounded like Greek to him, and even their jokes went over his head. The only one he remembered understanding was the one about what you get when you cross a Jewish princess with an S12 Mark 5—a computer that never goes down. And even then, it took him about ten seconds to get the punchline. To top things off, he was a Texan, which often made for strained social situations.

For some reason that had always escaped him, people from the mountain states had always had a prejudice against Texans. Just as in the old days, before the war, there had been a certain provincial rivalry between the east and west coasts, so people from states like New Mexico, Colorado and Wyoming had a tendency to look down on Texans. Perhaps it was because they bought up so much of their land. After the war, when Texas had seceded from what was left of the union to form its own government with its capital in Dallas, things grew even worse.

The country was in a terrible state. Washington, D.C., had been nuked into oblivion. The area for several hundred miles around it was still too hot to enter. New York had taken several missile strikes, as had Virginia, Boston and the area around the Cape in Florida, but the majority of the missile strikes had occurred out west, in places like Montana, Wyoming, Colorado, Idaho, New Mexico, Utah, and Nevada, where most of the missile silos were. The strikes in California had triggered disastrous earthquakes, which, combined with the virus, had taken a cataclysmic toll in human life. Most of Nevada was one giant radioactive hot spot, its borders patrolled by federal troops. There were also hot spots in central

and eastern Montana, in southern Idaho, northern Utah, throughout Wyoming, in eastern Colorado and just north of Denver,
as well as in Colorado Springs, which had been completely
levelled. In New Mexico, the entire area around Alamogordo
and White Sands practically glowed in the dark. The Jornada
del Muerto, that vast desert plain south of Socorro running
down to Hatch, was now truly the Journey of Death, as its
name implied. And the death toll brought about by the nuclear exchange was nothing compared to the loss of life
caused by the virus.

It had happened at the close of the twentieth century, just
as the new century was dawning. It was a dawn of death.
Terrorists acting in the name of Islam had somehow gotten
hold of a genetically-engineered virus, a deadly organism
created in a lab—no one knew where or when or by whom—
and intending to bring the western powers to their knees, they
had released it simultaneously in many of the major cities of
the world. However, they had vastly underestimated its viru-
lence and the incredible speed with which it spread.

Billions died within days of its release. The two major
superpowers, each thinking the other was responsible, had
immediately ordered retaliatory strikes, but only a small portion of their nuclear arsenals were ever actually launched.
Even as the dreaded order was given, missile-launch personnel keeled over at their posts as their fingers reached for the
deadly buttons, leaving armed missiles still standing in their
silos. Those that had not been destroyed were now inaccessi-
ble due to the radiation all around them. The entire human
race might have easily died out if the virus had not undergone
a rapid series of mutations.

The first and second mutations were only a little less
deadly than the original form. Those strains of the virus killed
more slowly, attacking the nervous system, mysteriously spar-
ing those lucky few who had somehow managed to acquire an
immunity. The third mutation, known as Virus 3, while not
immediately fatal, produced a carrier population called the
"screamers," who were left mentally and physically ravaged
by the disease. Within hours or even minutes of being in-

fected, they became hopelessly insane, their bodies breaking out in painful, hideous, suppurating sores. The psychopathic screamers would attack anything that moved, and most of those they came in contact with became infected like themselves. Because of this carrier population, Virus 3 was still a constant threat. There was no cure, and screamers were always shot on sight. Virus 4, the next mutation, destroyed the myelin sheaths of the nerve fibers and left its victims crippled, their nerves and muscles gradually deteriorating as the disease progressed. The dreadful cycle finally came to an end when the virus was transformed into a comparatively harmless organism that posed a threat only to the old and weak, those whose immune systems no longer functioned properly. It brought on something like pneumonia, not fatal in itself, but enough to weaken the body and leave it open to further infection. The victims usually died of complications within six months to a year.

By the time the awful cycle ran its course, the human population had been decimated and most of the world had been reduced to anarchy. In what had once been the United States, the crippled government was woefully decentralized, with its headquarters in New York and bases in the larger cities such as Boston, Philadelphia, Detroit, Chicago and Atlanta. Florida had become a semi-independent state, allied to the government, but Miami was a corrupt and freewheeling haven for pirates from the Gulf and the Caribbean, as well as every other sort of freebooter and hustler from Savannah to the Florida Keys. Most of the Southwest, with the exception of the larger cities, had regressed to the frontier lifestyle of the 1800s. Isolated pockets of civilization still existed in the northwestern states, but Nevada was a dead zone and no one knew what was going on in what remained of California. There was no contact with either Alaska or Hawaii, and though Canada and Mexico had sustained no missile strikes, their death toll from the virus had been staggering, and the government of both countries had collapsed.

In those places where there was no functioning authority, such as in much of the midwest, the south, and in certain areas of the northwest and the east coast, independent enclaves had arisen, many of them controlled by powerful criminal organizations that operated with impunity and preyed upon neighboring cities. The military had its hands full protecting outlying provinces, upon which the cities depended for their food, and most of the cities were now war zones, with their paramilitary police forces working fulltime to protect citizens from the savage predators in the ruins that surrounded them.

In such a climate of disaster, the act of Texas in setting up its own independent government was regarded by many as treason. The Republic of Texas had not turned its back on the rest of the country, and it extended full cooperation to the beleaguered government of the United States, but the Texans' attitude in wanting to control their own destiny was something that infuriated many people. Consequently, when he came to Los Alamos, Dev Cooper expected to encounter problems, but aside from some good natured ribbing, he was made to feel at home and he regretted leaving.

He also regretted giving up his work at Los Alamos, but the promise of a far more interesting and challenging assignment at Project Download headquarters in New York City had intrigued him. And, in some ways, he had had no choice. He had been selected, he was told, by the project director himself, Oliver Higgins, which had piqued his curiosity.

He knew that Higgins was not a cybernetics engineer. In fact, he was not even a scientist. He was the government administrator for the project, which meant that he was CIA. And Dev Cooper knew that meant his new assignment would be interesting.

All they had told him was that he would be working directly under Higgins at the Federal Building in New York, and the details of his job were classified. But they didn't have to tell him what the job was for him to make an educated guess. There was only one reason he could think of why they would want a man of his qualifications in New York. He was being assigned to Project Steele. And that meant there was no way he could refuse. What psychiatrist could resist the temptation to be a therapist to a man with a computer for a brain?

The results of Project Steele had only recently been released to the public, and though the actual details of the
project were still classified, there wasn't anyone with access
to a TV set who didn't know about Lt. Donovan Steele. The
news had been broken by Channel 7 in New York, and every
other station in the country had carried the story of the NYPD
Strike Force officer who had become a cyborg. He had seen
news footage of Steele in action and it was impressive, to say
the least.

Steele was a member of the Special Operations Division of
the NYPD, more popularly known as the Strike Force, an
elite police commando unit. Ambushed in the performance of
his duties, Steele had been shot up so badly that it was a
miracle he wasn't killed. The assassins had used fully automatic weapons loaded with armor-piercing and high-explosive
rounds, against which his body armor and riot helmet had
been scant protection. He arrived at the hospital in a coma,
his brain irreparably damaged. The prognosis had been grim.
He could be kept alive on life support, but he would remain a
vegetable.

However, shortly prior to being shot, Steele had partici-
pated in an experiment for Project Download. They had
requested a member of the Strike Force as a test subject for a
series of procedures to see if the knowledge and skills he had
acquired as a police commando could be downloaded from
his brain and programmed into a computer for transfer to
other test subjects. To facilitate this, Steele had undergone
surgery to install a biochip in his cerebral cortex that would
enable him to interface with the project computers. After he
was injured, he was brought to project headquarters where his
shattered body was repaired with organ transplants, sophisticated nysteel alloy prosthetics and polymer skin grafts, a
series of operations that reportedly took months.

His still-functioning implant enabled them to download the
data engrams from his damaged brain and program them into
a computer, where they were "debugged" with data engrams
downloaded from him previously, during the experiments.
When that procedure was completed, Steele's personality, his

identity reduced to software, was programmed into a cybernetic brain that had been installed inside a nysteel skull casing. The cybernetic unit was a prototype, the details of which were classified top secret. No one at Los Alamos had known anything about it or had even suspected its existence.

In the days prior to Dev's leaving for New York, it was all the project staff could talk about. They had inundated the project headquarters in New York with requests for transfers, and everyone he knew had handed him a resume, pleading with him to put in a good word for them when he arrived. The grapevine buzzed with rumors, and everybody wanted to know about the cybernetic brain and how it was connected to Steele's human nervous system. But that wasn't what interested Dev Cooper.

What Dev Cooper wanted to know about were the psychological effects on a man who came out of a coma to suddenly discover that he had a computer for a brain. A man who, by his own admission, still felt the same and thought the same, still had the same memories and sense of personal identity, but was plagued with the knowledge that his personality, or as he had put it, his soul, was contained in a computer. A man who, also by his own admission, was no longer sure if he was human.

He had a human heart beating in his chest. His lungs breathed air and there was blood flowing through his veins, but his skeletal system had been reinforced with nysteel, and there was a miniature fusion generator in his chest cavity powering his electronics. His human cells still held the same genetic template, and he was capable of having children, but the essence of his self was contained in sophisticated electronic circuitry. And how could that be considered human? What, Dev Cooper thought, must the man be *feeling*? A computer with emotions, encased in flesh and blood. It was a staggering idea. How on earth could he be coping with it?

The limo turned up First Avenue and drove through the gates of Federal Plaza. The flags of the United States—all save Texas, Dev noted—were fluttering from the flagpoles outside. They drove up to the entrance of what had once been the U.N. Secretariat Building, which now housed the offices of the Congress of the United States, as well as a number of government agencies. The Congress itself met in what had once been the General Assembly Building, the saddle-like structure connected to the Federal Building.

An escort of marines was waiting for him as he got out of the limo. They greeted him politely and very courteously walked him through the security checkpoint in the lobby where his identity was verified and he was carefully searched. He noticed, with some sense of disquiet, the guards in the lobby, all armed with fully automatic weapons. After he was passed through the checkpoint, he was escorted to the elevators and up to the twenty-second floor where the first sight that greeted him as the elevator doors slid open was the shield of the Central Intelligence Agency mounted on the wall.

"This way, please, doctor," one of the marines said, conducting him down the hall, past suites of offices to a black glass partition at the far end of the corridor. The gold letters on the wall read PROJECT STEELE. The marine pressed a small button on the intercom, and a voice responded from the speaker.

"Yes?"

"Dr. Devon Cooper to see Mr. Higgins."

"Has identity been verified?" the voice said.

"It has."

"One moment, please."

Dev noticed a security camera mounted overhead scanning him. He glanced up at it nervously.

"Come right in, Dr. Cooper."

The door buzzed and opened electronically. Dev stepped through into a waiting room that looked like one in a corporate office. Gray pile carpeting, chrome and black vinyl chairs, and a reception desk behind which sat a marine sergeant in dress blues. Four other marines stood around the room, at parade rest, each wearing a pistol in a white flap holster. The sixth man in the reception area was not in uniform. He was tall and slim, with dark hair graying at the temples, a cleft chin and alert dark eyes. He looked to be in his mid-forties.

He wore an elegantly tailored three-piece suit, dark gray with a fine charcoal stripe. His black shoes were highly polished, and his tie was a red silk foulard, perfectly knotted and held down with a small, tasteful gold stickpin. Button-down white shirt, french cuffs with small gold cufflinks. Tasteful. Understated. He looked slightly amused as he took in Dev's Stetson, shaggy brown hair and moustache, the western-cut tweed sport coat, the bolo tie lowered below the open collar, the faded jeans and the elkhide boots.

"Well, howdy, pardner," he said.

Dev winced.

"I'm Oliver Higgins. Welcome to New York."

Higgins held out his hand. Dev took it and they shook.

"Pleased to meet you, Mr. Higgins."

"My office is just down the hall," said Higgins. "How was your flight?"

"Okay, I guess," said Dev as they went down the hall. "Never did like flyin' much."

"Well, we'll give you some time to rest before you plunge in. We've arranged for you to stay in a furnished apartment on Sutton Place, just a short walk from here. Nice area. Secure. I'll have you dropped there after we're finished here. If there's anything you need, please don't hesitate to ask. I imagine you might want to pick up a few things."

"Like a suit and tie, you mean?" said Dev.

Higgins smiled. "Well, we don't really have a dress code here, but this isn't New Mexico. You might find yourself a bit conspicuous going about the city in those clothes. Especially the hat. The cowboys in this city don't ride horses. You'll be assigned an office and a secretary. She'll help you to familiarize yourself with the city, and she can arrange for anything you need. And I can recommend an excellent tailor who can provide you with a somewhat more, uh, regionally suitable wardrobe. The agency will pick up the tab. And you might want to get a haircut."

"That a condition of employment here?" asked Dev wryly.

"Merely a suggestion," Higgins said. "If you want to look like Wild Bill Hickock, doctor, it's no skin off my nose. But I'm not sure it's the image we'd like to project."

"Well, I wouldn't want to rock the boat," said Dev. "And I guess I could use some extra clothes. I only brought one suitcase. Mind if I keep the boots?"

"By all means, keep the boots," said Higgins with a smile. "We wouldn't want you to feel uncomfortable."

"Appreciate it."

Higgins opened the door to his office and they went inside. Dev looked around at the plush brown carpeting, the large mahogany desk, the dark wood panelling and the bar situated in the corner. There was a large console in the wall containing no fewer than ten video display screens.

"Nice," he said.

"Thank you," Higgins said. "Sit down. Drink?"

"Don't mind if I do," said Dev as he sat down in a leather upholstered armchair by the desk.

"Bourbon on the rocks, right?" Higgins said.

"That in my file?" Dev asked, raising his eyebrows.

"Oh, everything is in your file, doctor," Higgins said, walking over to the bar.

"That a fact?"

"We like to be thorough," Higgins said as he poured their drinks. He took Scotch for himself, straight up. "There isn't much about you we don't know. You're an expert horseman. You hunt and you're a crack shot with both rifle and pistol. You collect guns and you have a special fondness for revolvers, particularly old, single-action .45's. You have an IQ of 197, you're apolitical, you read philosophy and you're a student of western history. You wrote your thesis on Post-Traumatic Stress Disorder in the Aftermath of the Biowar. I read it. I found it cogently written, concise, well researched and thought out. You were married at nineteen, divorced at twenty because your wife discovered she wasn't quite ready to settle down with one man. No children, no desire to have any. Both parents dead, no living relatives. You're a workaholic, you drink a bit excessively, but you hold your liquor well. You don't smoke, you don't use drugs, although you've experimented with them in the past, and I understand you play a mean game of poker."

He handed Dev his drink.

"We'll have to play sometime," said Dev.

"My game is chess," said Higgins. "However, I don't think I'm in your league. Unlike you, I actually need to have a board in front of me."

Dev smiled. "You've done your homework."

"I always do," said Higgins, sitting down behind his desk. "I imagine you've surmised why you're here."

"I've been assigned to Project Steele?" said Dev.

Higgins nodded. "You'll be taking the place of Dr. Susan Carmody on the project staff," he said.

"Why did Dr. Carmody leave?" asked Dev.

"She didn't," said Higgins curtly. "She was killed."

"I'm sorry to hear that," Dev said. "Was it a, uh, job-related accident?"

"Not directly, no," said Higgins. "She got in the line of fire when an assassination attempt was made on Lt. Steele."

"Assassination attempt?" said Dev, frowning.

"Lt. Steele is a federal officer attached to Strike Force," Higgins said. "In the course of his duties, he's made some powerful enemies, notably one Victor Borodini, head of a large crime syndicate with headquarters in Cold Spring Harbor, on the north shore of Long Island. We've been having problems with the Borodini enclave for quite some time. He controls half the street gangs in no-man's-land, the area surrounding Midtown, where we are now. The street gangs are, to all intents and purposes, the law in no-man's-land, and Borodini provides them with arms and drugs, among other things. In return, he takes a cut of all their operations."

"Why don't you send the troops in and take care of him?" asked Dev.

"It's not as simple as all that," said Higgins. "For one thing, we can't really spare the troops. The city depends on the outlying provinces in areas like upstate New York and New Jersey for its supplies, and we need the troops there to protect them. Aside from that, the Borodini enclave is extremely well fortified and defended. They've got radar and surface-to-air missiles capable of taking out any choppers before they even get within range. A ground assault would require at least a full division to be successful. Unfortunately, that would be politically unfeasible.''

"Why's that?"

"The criminal enclaves on Long Island represent the only functioning authority out there," Higgins explained. "There are five principal enclaves. Borodini's, the Delano enclave in Brooklyn, the Pastori family in Queens, the Castellanos in Long Beach and The Brood, a large and heavily armed biker gang out in Montauk, on the eastern tip of the Island. Each enclave has a citizen population under its control, people who've had no choice but to turn to them for protection and a livelihood. The Brood, in particular, controls a large civilian population that makes up the agrarian communes in eastern Long Island and the fishing fleets along the shore. Any kind of assault on the enclaves would consequently result in significant loss of innocent civilian life. We don't have the military manpower, and the police here in the city have their hands full as it is. Up till now, the enclaves haven't presented a really significant problem, due to their rivalries, but Borodini has become the most powerful of the Long Island crime lords, and he wants nothing less than control of the city. If something isn't done about him soon, he might well get it.''

"How does Lt. Steele fit in?" asked Dev.

"He's got a personal score to settle with Victor Borodini," Higgins said. "It was Borodini's men who ambushed him and nearly killed him. We can't get to Borodini where he lives, but we can do everything we can to disrupt his operations in the city.''

"And that's where Steele comes in?" said Dev.

"Exactly," Higgins said. "I've turned him loose on the street gangs backed by Borodini. As a federal officer, he's not hampered by bureaucratic regulations governing the Strike Force, and he's free to hit and run, conducting urban guerrilla tactics against them. Our goal is to interfere with Borodini's operations enough to weaken him and make him vulnerable to the Delano family, which is the second most powerful enclave aside from The Brood, but The Brood doesn't really represent a threat to us. They're essentially self-sustaining, dealing with the enclaves for necessities they can't produce themselves. They don't conduct any criminal operations in the city, and so long as they leave us alone, we don't really care what they do.''

"So Steele disrupts Borodini's operations in the city and Borodini sends his soldiers after him," said Dev. He grimaced. "Sounds to me like you've sent him out to be a target."

"Precisely."

"Sort of a field test of his capabilities, is that it?" Dev said. "And if the prototype performs up to expectations, you get the funds to build yourself more cyborgs."

Higgins smiled. "I see you grasp the situation, Doctor. Building Steele was expensive. Consequently, the government wants to be certain we've perfected him before they allocate more funds for additional cyborgs. But they're extremely interested in what we're doing. Think what it could mean to have cyborg units in every major city. One of them could do the work of an entire assault team. With cyborg units attached to the military, we could free up a lot of manpower, enabling us to take some positive steps to bring back law and order and pull this country back together."

"I see," said Dev. "And how does Lt. Steele feel about all this?"

"He's holding up," said Higgins, "but he's had some difficulty in adjusting to the situation. That will be where you come in, Doctor. I can take care of his physical maintenance, but it will be your job to take care of his emotional stability."

"I'm no cybernetics engineer," said Dev. "I'm not qualified to debug computer programs."

"I know that," Higgins said. "We've got plenty of people on the project staff for that, but they're specialists in artificial intelligence, not *human* intelligence. And we're breaking totally new ground here. Steele's brain is a computer with a human personality. There's never been such a thing before. We've never had a computer with emotions. Consequently, we need a first rate psychotherapist to work with Steele and

supervise our cybernetics engineers in any program adjustments that might be necessary. Your qualifications in that
field are beyond reproach. What you do here will lay the
groundwork for the science of psychocybernetics for years to
come. I think you'll find this the most challenging and stimu-
lating task of your career.''

"I have no doubt of that," said Dev. "But my main
question is, just how much autonomy will I have? Like you
said, we're talkin' about breakin' entirely new ground here.
For me to do my job right, I'll need enough freedom to feel
my way around. And if Steele's goin' to be my patient, that
means my first responsibility will be to him. I can see where
things could get a little sticky.''

"I'm not sure I understand," said Higgins, frowning.

"Well, let me put it this way," Dev said. "Under ordinary
circumstances, the doctor/patient relationship would be completely confidential. But then these aren't exactly ordinary
circumstances, are they? Frankly, I've got no idea what the
law would say on this point, but let's set the law aside for the
sake of this discussion and simply cut to the chase. I could
say that my patient is a human being entitled to full civil
rights and confidentiality of treatment. On the other hand,
you could say he's a computer and my job is simply to fix up
any little glitches that might happen to crop up. Now we
could go back and forth about that till the cows come home,
but the fact is you already have access to his data engrams,
and I imagine you can run a download on him anytime you
like. So suppose something happens to come up that you
think requires some sort of adjustment to the program, but *I*
think it would constitute a violation of my patient's rights and
a threat to the integrity of his personality. What happens
then?''

"An excellent question, doctor," Higgins said. "Allow me
to set your mind at ease on that score. On the question of
doctor/patient confidentiality, you're quite correct in assum-
ing that we can pull a download on Steele anytime we choose.
However, I'm not really interested in knowing the specifics of
what the two of you might discuss in private. My only
concern when it comes to that is Steele's emotional stability.

And, quite frankly, I would prefer that to be handled in a traditional theraputic manner rather than making alterations to his programming, which would be very complicated and only a last resort.

"The details of this project are classified," he continued, "but we do have a highly visible profile, and the media would have a field day with the issue of cybernetic mind control. We're coming in for a certain amount of flak on that already, as I'm sure you must know from your work at Los Alamos. Consequently, when it comes to maintaining the integrity of Steele's personality, you will have full and absolute authority. You have my personal guarantee on that. You will attend all operational conference meetings, and no alterations will be made to Steele's programming without your express, written consent. Steele is a cyborg, not a robot. We're not interested in altering his personality in any way. We just want to make sure he stays healthy."

"Meanin' no offense," said Dev, "but would you mind lettin' me have that in writing?"

Higgins raised his eyebrows. "You're a careful man, Doctor."

"Well, as we say down in Texas," said Dev, "an oral agreement ain't worth the paper it's written on."

Higgins smiled. "All right. I'll have a signed statement to that effect drawn up for you. Will that be satisfactory?"

"I appreciate that," said Dev.

"In that case, Doctor, welcome aboard."

"Thanks. When do I get to meet my patient?"

"First thing in the morning, if you like," said Higgins. "But I thought you might want to familiarize yourself with his file first."

"Yes, I'd like that. Could I look it over tonight?"

"What time would be convenient?"

"What time?"

"I can't allow it to leave the premises," said Higgins, "but I can give you security access to it through the terminal in your apartment. I cannot, of course, allow you to pull a copy, but you can examine it as much as you like, anytime you like, providing you request clearance and a secure line first."

"I see you're a careful man yourself," said Dev. "But I can understand the reason for it. Would seven o'clock sharp be all right?"

"I'll arrange it," Higgins said. "And now, perhaps you'd like to see your office and meet your new secretary. If either doesn't meet with your approval, please let me know at once. Then perhaps you'd care to join me for lunch?"

"Thanks. I could do with a bite to eat. I didn't have time for breakfast. Is there anyplace a man can get himself some good heuvos rancheros?"

"What's that?" asked Higgins.

"Never mind," said Dev, "I'll settle for some steak and eggs."

Dev looked through the thick glass window into the room where Steele lay on his back, covered by a sheet up to his neck. They were in the fourth basement level, accessible only by a concealed elevator on the maximum security floor above it.

"Is he asleep?" asked Dev.

"In a manner of speaking," Higgins said. "He's on downtime."

"What do you mean, 'downtime'? You mean you turned him *off*?"

"Not exactly," Higgins said. "His cybernetic brain needs to be at least partially on line to maintain his organic functions. For Steele, downtime is the equivalent of being kept under sedation. In effect, he's sedated electronically. We've had him here ever since the assassination attempt, when Dr. Carmody was killed. He sustained some damage, and it was necessary to effect repairs. While we were at it, we also performed some upgrades on his prosthetics. That information hasn't been added to the file yet, but you'll be fully briefed. He exhibited some emotional distress over Dr. Carmody's death, so we've had him on downtime ever since."

"Was he very dependent on Dr. Carmody? The file doesn't indicate that."

"Steele's not really the dependent type," said Higgins. "They were lovers."

Dev stared at him with disbelief. "She allowed herself to

become *sexually involved* with her patient?'' He exhaled heavily. ''Jesus Christ.''

''They were both consenting adults, doctor,'' Higgins said.

''That's not the point. For a therapist to become sexually involved with a patient is a serious breach of professional ethics.''

''Well, I think it did him a lot of good,'' said Higgins. ''After what happened, his wife divorced him, taking their two children with her. Steele took it hard. His relationship with Dr. Carmody gave him something to focus on and reinforced his concept of his own humanity.''

''And now he's lost her as well,'' said Dev, shaking his head. ''I hardly think it did him any good, Mr. Higgins. How long has he been like this?''

''About two weeks. But for him, it'll be like waking up the morning after. I didn't want to bring him out of it until you got here.''

''What do you have to do to bring him out of it?'' asked Dev.

Higgins turned to Dr. Phillip Gates. ''Bring him on line,'' he said.

Gates sat down behind a computer console and started typing. A program came up on the screen. Gates typed in some commands, and seconds later, Steele began to breathe more deeply. His eyelids flickered open.

''All right, Doctor,'' Higgins said. ''Let's go in and meet your new patient.''

Dev glanced at him uneasily and followed him through the door.

''Good morning, Steele,'' Higgins said as they came in.

Steele simply gazed at him without expression.

''I'd like you to meet Dr. Devon Cooper, from Los Alamos. He'll be attached to project headquarters from now on, and he'll be working very closely with you.''

''Pleased to meet you, Lt. Steele,'' said Dev, holding out his hand.

Steele gazed at him without response.

Dev moistened his lips nervously and put his hand down. ''How do you feel?''

"You the new shrink?" said Steele.

"That's right."

"You didn't waste much time, did you?" Steele asked Higgins. "How long have I been down?"

"About two weeks," said Higgins.

For a moment, Steele lay still, without speaking. A small furrow appeared between his eyebrows.

"Something's different. Been tinkering again, Higgins?" he said.

He sat up suddenly and threw back the sheet. He was naked underneath. At first glance, he appeared perfectly normal. Solidly built, well muscled, with broad shoulders, dark hair and slate gray eyes. Dev knew that the eyes were artificial—sophisticated bionic optic units connected to a cybernetic optic nerve, with thermal imaging, laser designator and image enhancer systems built in. His limbs were nysteel alloy, sheathed in polymer skin, and his spine was reinforced with articulated nysteel sheathing. His ribs were also nysteel, as were his collarbone, scapula and shoulders. But to look at him, one could never tell. Only a close examination would reveal something different. Steele held up his arms and looked at them.

The lines in the skin on the inside of his wrists looked perfectly normal at first glance, but they were too wide and regular and on each hand, one of them extended all the way around across the back of the wrist. It wasn't immediately visible, and Dev might not have noticed it if it wasn't for the way Steele looked at them intently as he turned his hands over. Slightly below the center of each palm, there was a small, circular indentation in the polymer skin just above the heel of the hand.

"They detach," said Higgins.

Dev glanced at him with surprise.

"How?" asked Steele.

"The lock releases are slaved to your brain," Higgins said. "Except for Dr. Gates, who can activate the release mechanism while you're here by typing in a sequence of coded commands, you'll be the only one who can do it. As soon as he loads the program that will activate the upgrades, that is.''

"What goes on instead, hooks?" said Steele, dryly.

"You'll have a number of optional attachments," Higgins said, "all thought-controlled. You'll notice that your forearms and wrists are larger than they were before. Your hands are slightly bigger as well. We've installed a retracting, compensated 10 mm. gun barrel into your right forearm. The loading port is just below the crook of your right elbow. The magazine holds 15 rounds. You extend your arm to load one round at a time. The weapon will function with your hand either detached or locked in place. That dimple in your palm retracts to open your gun port. Once the barrel is exposed, you'll be able to attach a silencer if the situation calls for it. The system is of polymer/ceramic construction, so it will require no cleaning, and it will use caseless ammunition, so there will be no brass to be ejected. It will, however, require periodic maintenance from time to time.''

"What's in here?" asked Steele, looking at his left arm.

"A dart launcher," Higgins said. "It holds ten 45 mm. nysteel rocket darts, loaded through the port on the inside of your upper forearm, with an effective range out to 300 yards. The darts are electrically primed with a built-in millifuse, so they'll ignite within 20 to 30 feet of being launched hydraulically. And you'll have the option of tranquilizers, poison tip or explosive warhead. You can also launch ordinary titanium-tipped darts, non-rocket propelled, for a distance of 60 to 100 feet. And your optional attachments will also contain ports for those two weapons systems, though they won't resemble human hands.''

"Sort of like a vacuum cleaner with optional attachments," Steele said wryly.

"It should enable you to do a thorough job of cleaning up," said Higgins with a smile. "We've also made a few other modifications. We've used considerably stronger polymer skin grafting to make you more bulletproof, especially around your upper torso, to protect your organic parts. And we've reconstructed your jaw where you were shot using nysteel alloy. You also lost some teeth, so we replaced them all. You won't have to worry anymore about getting cavities."

Steele ran his tongue across his teeth.

"They look perfectly normal," Higgins said. "But they're polymer/ceramic. Virtually indestructible. However, if you don't want to have dragon breath from decaying food particles, you should still brush and floss regularly."

Dev followed the conversation with astonishment. But he also watched Steele carefully to see how he was taking it.

"Did you do a tune-up and an oil change while you were at it?" Steele asked.

Higgins smiled. "Absolutely. You're good for another 50,000 miles."

"Where are my clothes?"

"In the cabinet over there," said Higgins.

Steele got up, unselfconscious in his nakedness, walked over to the cabinet and started getting dressed.

"When do I get to leave here?"

"After the upgrade program has been loaded and you've been checked out on the new systems," Higgins said. "But Dr. Cooper will want to spend some time with you first."

Steele zipped up his dark blue coveralls and glanced at Dev. "You sure you want this job, Doctor?" he said. "The last person who had it died."

"Yes, I've heard," said Dev. "I understand that you and Dr. Carmody were very close. I'm sorry about what happened."

Steele glanced at Higgins. "Yeah. So am I."

"Well, I'll leave the two of you to get acquainted," said Higgins. He glanced at Steele. "And later on, there's someone else you might like to meet. Someone who'll also be working with you closely."

"Who?" asked Steele.

"A gentleman by the name of Ice," said Higgins with a smile.

Steele gave him a sharp look. "Ice is *here*?"

"He's in protective custody," said Higgins, "but you wouldn't know it from the way he acts. He thinks he's staying in some fancy hotel with room service. The man eats like a horse."

"Ice?" said Dev. "What is that, some sort of code name?"

"It's a street name, Doctor," Steele said. "Ice is the man Victor Borodini's soldiers were after when they shot me up." He paused briefly. "He was the last man to see me as I was, though we didn't actually meet face-to-face."

"Well, now you'll have that chance," said Higgins. "I think you'll find him an interesting man, Steele. In some ways, the two of you have much in common."

"What kind of deal did you make with him?" asked Steele.

"Full immunity, in return for his cooperation in helping us against Victor Borodini. He knows a great deal about his operations out in no-man's-land."

"I'll bet he does," said Steele. "Come on, doctor, let's go someplace where we can talk and get this over with. I've got things to do."

The congressional lounge on the third floor of the Federal Building had been the delegates' bar during the days of the United Nations. It was situated on the north side of the building. The entire north wall was glass, affording a panoramic view of the rose garden and the buildings beyond it. In the distance stood the crumbled remains of the Queensboro Bridge. The lounge was large and spacious, filled with low coffee tables and comfortable reading chairs upholstered in black leather. The long bar was on the side opposite the windows, and to its left, between the bar and the entrance, a huge tapestry hung on the wall, depicting the Great Wall of China. This early in the day, there was hardly anybody there, and after a nod of greeting to the security guards stationed at the entrance, Steele led Dev over to one of the tables near the windows. A waiter came and took their order. Steele ordered black coffee. Dev asked for the same.

"I figured we could talk here," Steele said. "Congressmen never get up this early, so it's pretty quiet this time of day. Unless you feel like going upstairs for breakfast."

"Already had mine. What about yourself? You haven't eaten for two weeks."

"Not really hungry. They feed me through a tube in my throat while I'm on downtime," Steele said. "Some kind of mush. I haven't got the faintest idea what it tastes like. I never eat breakfast anyway. I only have coffee in the morning. Where're you from, originally?"

"El Paso."

"I thought the accent was Texan. El Paso. That's near the Mexican border, isn't it?"

"Right smack on it," Dev said. "Ever been there?"

"No, I've never left New York. Lived here all my life. What's it like?"

"El Paso? Well, it's different. Lots warmer, for one thing. And prettier, to my way of thinkin'. We didn't take any missile damage from the war, though we lost a lot of people to the virus. It's a fair-sized city, though not like this. Not as many people. Not as much crime, though we've got our share."

"You have much trouble with the border?"

"Some, but not as much as you might think," said Dev. "The border isn't really closed. The city's more than half Mexican, anyway. Those people have it pretty hard down there. Most of their population died off from the virus. We get some screamers and bandits comin' across every now and then, but the Border Patrol's pretty good at takin' care of them. Except for the big drug traders, they're not very well armed."

"What about the drugs?"

"We made 'em legal," Dev said. "It solved a lot of problems. We register our addicts. They start hurtin', they can come into a clinic, show their card and get taken care of. It's lots cheaper than havin' them out commitin' crimes to get their fix. And it eliminated the criminal drug trade. There's just no money in it anymore. The drug lords down in Mexico pretty much leave us alone. They deal with the freebooters in the Gulf who come up north and sell to you folks. We actually have more trouble from our American borders."

"Higgins said you came out from Los Alamos."

"I was on the staff at Project Download there."

"I didn't know there was a branch in New Mexico."

"It's a big project. There are research branches in several different cities," Dev said.

"How'd you get involved in it?"

"They were looking for someone who specialized in abnormal and stress-related psychology," said Dev. "That's my field. There's really no such thing as cybernetic psychiatry, so I guess they were looking for someone who'd worked with some unusual cases and could manage to fit in. I was practicing out of a psychiatric hospital in El Paso, and one day I got a phone call, asking if I'd be interested in working on a classified government research project. I was intrigued and one thing sorta led to another."

"What made you want to become a shrink?" asked Steele.

"Well, at the risk of sounding corny," Dev replied, "I wanted to help people. I found out early on that I was good at it. Even as a kid, my friends always came to me with their problems. I guess I listen good."

"You haven't really asked me any questions," Steele said.

"You seemed to have some of your own. I'm not in any rush," said Dev. "What do your friends call you?"

"Steele."

"Mine call me Dev."

"Does that mean we're friends?" asked Steele sardonically.

"You don't much like shrinks, do you?" Dev asked.

"No, not really."

"Mind if I ask why?"

"Most shrinks I've met can never turn it off," said Steele. "They're always poking around, trying to figure out what makes people tick so they can fit them into convenient categories and slap a label on them. And I don't like being pigeonholed."

Dev nodded. "Well, I suppose you've got a point there," he said. "I'm afraid a lot of us tend to do that sort of thing. Occupational hazard, I guess."

"But you don't do it, is that it?"

"I try not to. But it isn't always easy. In some ways, I guess it's a bit like bein' a cop."

"How's that?" asked Steele, frowning.

"Well, when you spend your life doin' a certain thing, like bein' a policeman, you develop certain patterns of behavior that are an inevitable result of the job. You don't really look at people the same way other folks do. You tend to watch for certain things, little telltale signs you've learned to pick up on the job, signs that tell you things about those people. Signs you've learned to read because they could give you important information. Things like body language. Do the eyes shift a bit when the person's talkin' to you? That could mean that they're lyin'. Do they pause before answerin' a question or do they answer right away? Do they reply too quickly? Is there a sign of perspiration on the upper lip? Do they pick up their breathin' slightly? Do the hands move nervously? Things like that. After a while, I suppose a cop tends to look at just about everyone as a potential criminal." Dev shrugged. "That doesn't mean he thinks they are. He's just learned to watch for certain things. He can't help it. He can't really turn it off, either."

Steele smiled. "Good point," he said.

"Categories can be useful, like generalities, because some folks just seem to fit 'em," Dev said. "Doesn't mean that everybody does. I try to keep in mind that just because I've got a piece of paper that says I know a lot about certain kinds of human conditions, doesn't mean I know it all. I watch out for easy answers. I don't really think there are any."

"That's funny," Steele said. "Someone else once told me almost exactly the same thing."

"Dr. Carmody?"

Steele shook his head. "No. A man named a Liam Casey. He's a priest." Steele smiled. "You'd like him. He wears cowboy boots, too."

"He a westerner?"

"No, born and raised in New York City. But he's different. I suppose there's a bit of the cowboy in him. He's a good friend." Steele paused. "I haven't got that many."

"You mean lately?"

"Especially lately," Steele said.

Dev said nothing.

"My best friend was killed the same time I was injured," Steele went on. "His name was Mick Taylor. He was my partner." He paused. "Seems like anytime I get close to someone, they either leave or get killed."

"You mean your wife," said Dev. "Leavin' you, that is."

"In some ways, she left me a long time ago," said Steele, looking out the window. "Just that I never really noticed."

"And Susan Carmody died because someone was tryin' to kill you," said Dev.

Steele nodded.

"How does that make you feel?"

"How do you *think* it makes me feel? How would it make *you* feel?"

"I suppose I'd feel angry. And I might feel responsible."

Steele shook his head. "I don't feel responsible," he said. "But I know who is."

"Victor Borodini?"

"That's right. And I intend to make him pay."

"Think that'll make it right?"

"I'm not obsessed with it, if that's what you mean," said Steele. "But it's something that needs doing. It won't bring Mick and Susan back, and maybe it won't make me feel any better, but it'll make things right."

"Revenge will make things right?"

"No," said Steele. "Not revenge. Justice."

"Well, I'll drink to that," said Dev.

They saw a lot of each other during the following week, and Steele discovered that Dev Cooper wasn't like any psychiatrist he'd ever met before. For one thing, they never had formal therapy sessions in Dev's office or anywhere else. They talked casually over their meals, over drinks or coffee and during Steele's training sessions, while he was checked out on his new upgrades. Dev Cooper was a good listener. Steele had braced himself for all the expected questions, but Dev simply never asked them. He had never once referred to Steele's cybernetic brain nor, for that matter, did he ask any questions beyond the sort of things that could crop up in any casual conversation. But Steele realized early on that Dev Cooper didn't miss much. He had an easygoing, folksy way about him that was both disarming and deceptive. He didn't push, he didn't pry, but he listened carefully to everything that Steele *didn't* say, as well as everything he said. And he had a few surprises for Steele, too.

While Steele was practicing on the range with his new, built-in weapons systems, Dev had commented favorably on his shooting, and Steele had explained how, with his computer brain and built-in laser designator, it was virtually impossible for him to miss. And then, playfully, he had suggested that Dev give it a try and handed him a police issue 9 mm. semiauto. Dev had checked the weapon competently, then he stepped up to the line, and using a modified Weaver combat stance, he had drilled the X-ring, with only one flyer in the eight ring out of 15 shots.

"Where the hell'd you learn to shoot like that?" Steele had asked, impressed.

"Hey, son, I'm from Texas," was Dev's answer.

Dev wasn't present when Steele finally met Ice, though Steele felt certain that Dev would hear their conversation. Higgins was very big on hidden surveillance devices. They had Ice "on ice" in a room on Level B-2, one of the maximum security floors. There were two armed guards stationed outside the door. It was a comfortable room, though spartan, with nothing in it but a bed, a reading chair, a table, a portable radio and a television set. Ice was watching TV when Steele came in.

It was the first time Steele had ever actually met him face-to-face. He thought back to their only other meeting, on the day that Mick had died and his own life was changed forever.

Capt. Jake Hardesty of the Strike Force had received a call

from a man claiming to be Ice, the leader of the Skulls, the most powerful street gang in the no-man's-land just north of Midtown. No law enforcement officer had ever actually seen Ice, though there wasn't a cop in New York City who didn't know about him. Under his leadership, the Skulls had become a well organized machine, dominating all the other gangs located on their turf and wiping out all those who would not accept their leadership. But lately, the Skulls had experienced dissension in their ranks. They had been approached by representatives of the Borodini enclave with a business proposition that their war council had found difficult to refuse.

It was the same deal that Borodini had offered to the most powerful street gangs in the south end of Manhattan, the Green Dragons and the Chingos. The Borodini enclave would supply them with arms, drugs and other commodities in return for a percentage of their action, a percentage that seemed very reasonable. But there was a catch. Doing business with Victor Borodini meant taking orders from Victor Borodini, and that was something Ice was not willing to do. However, he had been outvoted by the other members of his war council, and the leadership of the Skulls passed to his deputy, Akeem. Ice hadn't taken kindly to being deposed as leader of the Skulls. He had contacted the Strike Force, wanting to set up a meeting to discuss a proposition. Hardesty sent Steele.

With Mick Taylor covering him from their armored unit parked outside and backup units posted several blocks away, Steele had gone in to meet with Ice alone. They met in an abandoned storefront, but Ice had stayed back in the shadows, out of sight. His proposition was a simple one. Borodini had scheduled a meeting with the warlords of the Skulls, the Dragons and the Chingos. The man himself would be there. Ice would tell them where the meeting would take place. All he wanted in return was for the Strike Force to take Borodini out of the picture, along with Akeem and the other warlords who'd deposed him. Steele didn't like the idea of doing Ice's dirty work for him, but he knew it was not an offer that the Strike Force could ignore. A chance at Victor Borodini and the warlords of the most powerful gangs in no-man's-land was simply too good to pass up. Only before Ice could reveal the location of the meeting, Borodini's men had struck.

Steele could still hear his partner's scream as their unit was blown up and Mick leaped out in flames. There was a second explosion, and Mick was hurled forward by the blast, to land motionless on the street. And then Borodini's soldiers opened up with everything they had. By the time the backup units arrived, it was too late. Mick had died and Steele was near death himself, in a coma with irreparable brain damage, his body chewed up by armor-piercing bullets. When he woke up, he was a cyborg. And he hadn't seen Ice since that day.

Ice reclined on the bed, dressed in black slacks and a black tank top. He picked up the remote control and turned off the TV as Steele came in. He was a giant of a man, well over six feet tall, and almost 300 pounds of solid muscle without an ounce of fat. His massive chest was about 60 inches around, and his bulging arms were larger than most men's thighs. He was clean-shaven and his head was shaved as well. He wore dark sunglasses and a gold chain around his neck with a small golden skull dangling from it. When he spoke, he sounded like the voice of doom.

"Well, well," he said, "if it ain't Lt. Steele. Been wonderin' when you'd show up."

"Hello, Ice," said Steele. "I thought Borodini's men took care of you."

"Not me, police man. But I hear they took care of you *real* good."

"Yeah," said Steele. "Only they didn't quite finish the job."

Ice got off the bed and came around to stand in front of Steele. He towered over him. The two men sized each other up.

"Last time I saw you, you was shot up pretty bad. Looks like they fixed you up," said Ice. "Way I hear it, you one mean machine now."

Steele grimaced. "You always wear those shades?"

Ice smiled and took them off. His eyes were like anthracite. Cold, dark and hard.

"Been coolin' my heels for three weeks and then some, waitin' for you to be up and around," said Ice. "This damn room been gettin' smaller every day."

"Would you rather be out there in the streets, taking your chances with Borodini's contract on you?" Steele asked.

"I'd rather be out there *doin'* somethin' about it," Ice said. "When we gettin' out of this place?"

"We?" said Steele.

"You and me, police man," Ice said. "That's the deal. *Cooperation.* Like I told Higgins, I ain't gonna sit here, singin' like some bird, while someone else goes out and checks out all the leads I give 'em. This here's a *hands on* proposition. Anything you get, I want a piece of. All except for Victor Borodini. I want *that* man all to myself."

"You're not in any position to make demands, Ice," Steele told him.

"Who gonna *stop* me? You?"

"Maybe, if you rattle my chain too hard," said Steele. "But I wouldn't really need to. If Higgins wanted to, he could open you up like a tin can. Give you a little shot and you'd tell him everything you know with a great big stupid smile on your face. In fact, I wonder why he didn't do that."

"I *tell* you why, police man. Because it ain't what I know so much as *who* I know and who I can *get* to," Ice said. "I still got friends out there. Connections. Knowin' who they are ain't gonna help your people. They need me to get to 'em. And I need you to balance off Borodini's muscle. We need each other, Steele. You scratch my back, I scratch yours."

"If I wanted a partner," Steele said, "you'd be the *last* one that I'd pick. I work alone."

"Your man Higgins might have somethin' to say about that," Ice said.

"I'll take it up with him."

"You do that. But you go out to no-man's-land alone, you won't find nuthin' without someone to steer you in the right direction, get the right doors open. You think about it, Steele," Ice said, getting back up on the bed. "Give it some thought. But don't take too long about it. It gettin' real close in here."

He put his shades back on and turned on the TV.

"It's out of the question," Steele said. "There's no way I'm going to work with that man."

Higgins sat behind his desk. Dev Cooper sat in one of the armchairs across from it. He didn't participate in the discussion, he simply watched and listened.

"I think you ought to reconsider," Higgins said. "Ice could be a definite asset to this operation. He knows his way around and he could—"

"Forget about it," Steele said, interrupting. "You want to make a deal with him for what he knows, that's up to you, but I'm not working with him and that's final."

For a moment, Higgins said nothing. Then he took a deep breath and let it out slowly.

"It's not your option, Steele," he said in a measured tone. "I can understand your objections to working with Ice. He is, after all, a wanted criminal, but the police have certainly worked with criminals before. You've used informers, you've cut deals. This is no different. Ice was the number one man among the Skulls for many years, and before he was forced out, he managed to acquire a great deal of knowledge about Borodini's operations in Harlem. He's got contacts and he's got resources out in no-man's-land that we don't have access to. I'm not asking you to like the man or even trust him. But I do expect you to work with him. If you insist on being uncooperative, I could easily have Dr. Gates program you with an imperative that would leave you with no choice, but I would prefer not to have to do that. Unless, of course, you force my hand. I trust we understand each other."

Steele gave him a long, hard look.

"*Do* we understand each other?"

The corner of Steele's mouth twitched. "Yeah," he said.

"Good. I've made it clear to Ice that he will be under your authority." Higgins smiled faintly. "He's about as happy about that as you are. But he's got a score to settle with Victor Borodini, and I think we can count on that to keep him in line."

"What if he gets *out* of line?" asked Steele.

"It will be your job to see that he doesn't," Higgins said. "I think you can handle that."

"Right," said Steele flatly.

"We've repaired the damage done to your apartment," Higgins said. "And I've had the security beefed up, so there won't be any repetition of what happened last time. We've informed the media that after that helicopter attack, we're not taking any chances, and any of their choppers that intrude upon the airspace around your penthouse will be fired upon. Under the circumstances, since that chopper that Borodini's men used was hijacked from Channel 4, they were very understanding. I've also arranged for separate quarters for Ice in the same building. When he's not with you, I'd kind of like to have him where we can keep an eye on him."

"Anything else?" said Steele.

"I guess that about covers it," said Higgins. "As of now, you're back on active duty."

"Fine," said Steele.

He turned and left the room.

"You could've handled that a little better," Dev said, after Steele had gone.

"Steele's a federal officer, Doctor," Higgins said. "And I expect him to follow orders."

"I'm not arguin' with that," said Dev. "But it was a mistake to threaten him with a programmed imperative."

"That is one of our options, Doctor," Higgins said, "and if it becomes necessary, I intend to use it. We've got too much invested in Steele to risk letting him become too independent. He's got to learn to accept what he is."

"Oh, he's accepted it, all right," said Dev, "but acceptin' something and learnin' to live with it are two very different things. All things considered, he's handlin' what happened to him remarkably well, but he's a long way from havin' learned to live with it. And I'm not sure he ever will. He hides it well, but he's under an incredible amount of stress. That worries me. That worries me a lot."

"You think he might have problems?" Higgins asked.

"He's already *got* problems," Dev said. "The question is, can he learn to deal with them? I don't know. I'd be a whole lot happier if I could spend more time with him."

"I can understand that, Doctor," Higgins said, "but I need Steele on the streets. You assured me he was fit for duty."

"I gave you my *best* assurances," said Dev, "but that's still no guarantee there won't be any problems. He's a man with human emotions locked inside a cybernetic brain. There's really no way to predict how he might respond." He paused. "I really just don't know. I've never been faced with anything like this before. You tell me. What happens when a computer has a nervous breakdown?"

3

Steele's home on Park Avenue near East 79th Street was a security building housing government personnel. Many of the buildings in Midtown were staffed with private security, paid for by the residents to protect their homes and businesses. In the aftermath of the Bio-War, private security had become a growth industry. Officially, it was regulated by the New York Police Department, but in practice, the NYPD simply didn't have the resources to do the job properly.

There were a number of large, bonded, private security companies in Midtown staffed by trained personnel that were licensed by the city, many of them ex-cops and retired military personnel, but the city didn't have the manpower to keep tabs on all the companies, some of which were little more than fly-by-night concerns operating on a shoestring budget. In many cases, especially among those citizens of Midtown who were less well off, the building residents could not even afford to hire one of the less reputable companies, so they did the job themselves or hired "independents." Consequently, private security could range from personnel who had retired from the police force or the military to burly dockworkers and warehousemen to ex-gang members and criminals who had gone straight. In some cases, not entirely straight.

In many ways, the situation was not unlike that on the frontier in the 1800s, when ranchers often hired "stock detectives" and "regulators" to protect their herds from rustlers. It was often difficult, if not impossible, to check the backgrounds of the people that they hired, and many of them

didn't even bother, so long as they could do the job. Predict-
ably, there were problems, and it was much the same in
Midtown. There were accidental shootings, cases where the
security guards themselves burgled the residences they were
hired to protect, fights, rapes, killings, fueds among competing security outfits, and it was the NYPD's unhappy duty to
step in and try to clean them up. But in a city bordered on all
sides by areas of lawlessness, the citizenry wouldn't stand for
any laws limiting their rights to hire their own protection or to
carry guns themselves. Crime was rampant, and no one knew
better than the cops that they couldn't do the job alone.

With the population decimated by the virus, many of the
buildings in the city stood completely empty, havens for
criminals and derelicts and screamers. Only a small portion of
the subway lines still ran beneath the Midtown area, leaving
the vast majority of the tunnels empty, collapsing and falling
into disrepair, giving shelter to all sorts of human refuse who
scuttled in the dark and came up to prey upon the citizens.
The law, what there was of it, could most often be found at
the barrel of a gun, and it would be years before the city's
population increased to a point where the residents could
exercise a greater semblance of control over their environment. In the meantime, they existed in an urban jungle,
teeming with predators, with only isolated areas providing
any measure of safety. New York, a city that once never
slept, now locked its doors and steel shutters tightly every
night, counting on those who made their living with a gun to
keep them safe.

The men on duty at Steele's building were all federal
agents, each armed with a 9 mm. semiautomatic pistol and a
4.7 mm. battle rifle that fired both shotgun rounds and caseless
ammunition. Its select fire system gave the shooter choice of
semiautomatic, three-round burst or full auto. The security
personnel all wore civilian clothing, but they had body armor
on underneath their shirts and ties. Most of the people living
in the building worked at Federal Plaza or in city administration, and it had been a long time since there was any trouble
in the building or its immediate environs. As a result, though

they were pros, the security officers had grown a bit complacent. The helicopter assault on Steele's penthouse changed all that.

They were all stung by the death of Dr. Susan Carmody and by Steele's own close brush with death. The whip had cracked and security procedures were tightened. They all knew Steele by sight, but even though they'd been briefed about Ice, they still checked with project headquarters before admitting him into the building.

They took the elevator up to Steele's penthouse apartment, originally used to house visiting V.I.P.'s and maintained by the agency. It was a luxurious suite, with dove gray carpeting and furniture upholstered in a matching shade. There was a bar in the corner of the living room, panelled in gray marble, and paintings on the walls, abstract art that Steele didn't particularly care for, but he left them where they were. It was a place for him to sleep, no more. It didn't really feel like home. Home had once been an apartment that he'd shared with Janice and their children, but in the last months of their rocky married life, that had ceased to feel like home as well. The pain of their separation was still with him.

Janice had never been able to accept what Steele did to earn a living. Their relationship had been based on a powerful physical and emotional attraction, but the two of them had almost nothing else in common. Janice had craved stability. Life as a cop's wife did not offer much of that. They had started drifting apart after a year of marriage, and then Jason had been born. For a time, he had strengthened their relationship, but then it started to get shaky once again. Then Cory's birth had reinforced it, but it wasn't long before things began to go downhill once more. Their passion for each other was strong to the end, but it took more than passion to make a marriage work, and though they had stayed together for the sake of the children, each year saw them growing farther and farther apart.

After Steele was shot down and transformed into a cyborg, it was more than Janice could deal with. While he lay in the basement of the Federal Building, undergoing the long and complex series of operations that had made him what he was now, Janice had divorced him and left the city, taking the children with her. He had no idea where she was. Though she had never seen him after he had received his cybernetic brain, she had obtained a restraining order against him, preventing him from trying to contact her or the kids in any way. In her own words, according to Mick Taylor's sister, Shelley, she had not wanted her children to have ''some kind of robot'' for a father.

And the only other woman Steele had ever come to care for was now dead as a result of an attempt upon his life. He stepped out onto the balcony and looked down at the spot where she had fallen, struck down by machinegun bullets fired from a helicopter. The floor had been resurfaced. There was no longer any sign of blood or bullet damage. But Steele could still see it, could still see her ruined body lying there in a sea of red, her eyes staring up sightlessly at the sky.

''That where the lady doctor died?'' said Ice softly from behind him.

''Yeah,'' said Steele. He looked out across the city and took a long, deep breath.

''She someone special to you, huh?''

''Yeah,'' said Steele. ''She was someone special.''

''Make no difference to her what you were,'' said Ice.

Steele turned around. ''I think it made a difference,'' he said. ''She was one of the people who made me what I am. Maybe because of that, or maybe in spite of it, but she was able to accept it.'' He paused. ''Which is a lot more than I can say for myself.''

''Hey, you be what you are, man,'' Ice said. ''Ain't no use askin' questions, ain't gonna change *nuthin'*.''

Steele smiled. ''Is it really that simple for you?''

''Life too short to be agonizin' over who you are,'' said Ice. ''Man takes what he got and runs with it. Ain't no other way I know.''

''I guess there's something to be said for that,'' said Steele. ''You want to go check out your new apartment?''

''No hurry,'' Ice said. ''I been itchin' to get out for a long time. When we gettin' started?''

"Before we do, let's get something straight between us right away," said Steele. "Working with you wasn't my idea."

"I hear that. But the man gave you no choice."

"That's right. So even though I'm not exactly thrilled about it, we're going to have to work together. But I'm going to call the shots. Understood?"

"I hear that, too," Ice said, "but when we out in Harlem, you best let *me* do all the talkin'. Ain't no brother gonna give the time of day to no white police man."

"All right," said Steele. He walked back into the apartment and went over to a wooden cabinet. He opened it to reveal an arms locker. "You're going to need a piece," he said. "But if you so much as *think* about pulling it at the wrong time, I'm going to make you eat it."

Ice chuckled. "Man don't mince no words," he said, walking over to the cabinet. He looked inside. "My, my, my. The candy store is open."

He reached inside and took out an old Model 1911-A1 .45 Colt semiauto.

"Not that one," Steele said.

Ice glanced at him curiously.

"That one's mine," said Steele. "It was my father's. Put it back."

Without a word, Ice replaced the pistol on its hooks. He took out another gun, a large, stainless steel .44 magnum automatic with a six-inch barrel, a wrap-around rubber grip, ambidextrous safety and combat sights and trigger. It weighed a hefty 60 ounces and held a 10-shot clip.

"This one do just fine," he said.

"You'll find a holster rig for it in the drawer there," said Steele. "Spare clips in the drawer beneath it."

Ice took out a cordura shoulder holster rig, four spare magazine clips and a box of ammo.

"What about a rifle?" he said.

"That's all you get," said Steele. "For now, anyway. Later on, we'll see. Like you said, a man takes what he's got and runs with it."

"Where we runnin' to?" asked Ice.

"To your old stomping grounds," said Steele, walking over to the bar. "What do you drink?"

"Got any vodka?"

"How do you take it?"

"Straight, on the rocks."

Steele poured their drinks then brought them over to the coffee table by the couch.

"You said you knew a lot about Borodini's operations out in Harlem," he said. "Okay, then. Fill me in."

The gypsy cab turned right off 125th Street, heading toward the waterfront along the Hudson River. Steele and Ice both sat in the back while the driver, a grizzled, skinny old black man in a black leather jacket and floppy leather cap, drove the scarred and battered cab at about thirty miles an hour, carefully keeping an eye on the streets around them.

"Slim and me go way back," Ice explained. "Slim on the war council of the Skulls when I joined as a kid. Took me under his wing and taught me. Ain't that right, Slim?"

"Took a shitload o' teachin', too," said Slim from the front seat, his voice sounding hoarse and raspy. Steele guessed he was around 65 years old. "Damn kid *always* gettin' his ass in trouble. Like now. With a contract on 'is head and runnin' with some honky cop."

"This honky cop gonna help me get the man who put the contract out on me," Ice said. "He a friend of mine, so you be polite."

"Just the two of you take on Victor Borodini?" Slim said. He snorted. "I be at your funeral. You want to kill yourselves, why not let me turn you in? I could use a fast twenty-five grand."

"You're worth twenty-five thousand to Victor Borodini?" Steele asked Ice. "He must want you real bad."

"Not half as bad as he want you," said Ice with a grin. "You worth a cool half mill. People down here sell their own mothers for lot less than that."

"Half a mill?" said Slim, glancing up in the rearview mirror. "You that cyborg cop?"

"Yeah, that's me," said Steele.

"Shoot," said Slim, "I ain't never been near so much money in my life. Look, what say you let me drive you out to Long Island and turn you over to the Borodinis, save you the trouble of committin' suicide?"

"What you do with all that money?" asked Ice.

"Buy me a boat an' sail away to some damn island," Slim said. "Warm beaches an' young brown girls to take care o' me in my old age."

"They take care of you, all right," said Ice. "Man your age, they do you in for sure."

"Yeah, but what a way to go," said Slim with a smile.

"Don't let him fool you," Ice said. "Slim got himself a stable of fine young foxes. They take care of him real good."

"He's a pimp?" said Steele, with surprise.

"I calls it 'entertainment broker,' " Slim said hoarsely. "White folks from Midtown want some entertainment, I provides it, they get broker." He cackled.

"Slim one of the few independents in this part of town," said Ice, "on account of he used to be a Skull. The bloods leave him alone to run his own action. Some people don't like it, but ain't nuthin' they can do about it."

"They can try," said Slim. "I'm ready for 'em. Like that young blood, Akeem. Wants me to give the Skulls a cut of my action now. *Me*! I was on the council when he was no more'n a nasty gleam in some damn nigger's eye! Young bloods nowadays got no respect, no style. Takin' orders from some *whitebread* out on Long Island. *Shee-it!*"

"So Akeem is still alive," said Steele.

"No thanks to you," said Ice. "He got messed up bad that time you hit the Skulls. Took some shrapnel from one of your grenades. Still carryin' round some pieces. Cut his pretty face up an' made him lose an eye. You *not* one of his favorite people."

"He's not one of mine, either," Steele said.

It was growing darker, but Slim turned his lights off as the cab slowly turned into a side street near the piers. They were in a desolate area of the city, nothing but old abandoned warehouses and crumbled ruins. There was not a sign of life. Slim pulled the cab over to the curb and shut the engine off.

"This it?" asked Steele, looking around.

"We walk from here," said Ice. "Warehouse down at the far end of the block. There be guards posted."

"Skulls?" asked Steele.

"Mostly," Ice said. "Borodini got some men stationed there, maybe three or four. All others be Skulls."

"How many?"

Ice shrugged. "Maybe ten, twelve. Don't know for sure. Could be more, since that new shipment come in."

"They gotta lot of firepower there," said Slim. "You *sure* you don't want to go call in for some backup?"

"No," said Steele. "I'm going to take care of this myself. And I want to be sure that Borodini hears about it. Ice, you wait here with Slim."

"Like hell," said Ice, opening the car door. "I ain't no tour guide, police man. Like I said, this here a *hands on* proposition."

"I don't want to argue," Steele said. "This isn't a safe area. Somebody should stay behind with Slim."

"Slim take care of himself," said Ice.

Steele heard the sound of a bolt being drawn back. He glanced at Slim. The old man was holding a .45 caliber machine pistol.

"You not back in half an hour, brother, I'm gone," said Slim.

"Fair enough," said Ice. He glanced at Steele. "We goin', or are you an' me gonna stand here an' argue some?"

Steele stared at him for a moment, then nodded. "All right. But if you go down, I'm not stopping for you."

"I hear you. Let's do it."

They moved off down the street, hugging the buildings, then cut through an alley and circled round behind the warehouse. From the outside, it looked no different from the other buildings that surrounded it. The entire area appeared deserted. There was no sign of any guards posted.

"Boys must be sleepin' on the job," said Ice as they

approached the back of the warehouse. He glanced around at the adjoining buildings, up at the roof, but there was no sign of anyone.

"Maybe they figured no one would be crazy enough to hit this place," said Steele.

"They figure wrong," said Ice.

As they spoke, a door at the side of the building opened, and two young black men in gang colors stepped out into the alley. They lit up cigarettes. Steele and Ice drew back into the shadows, flattening themselves up against the building wall.

There was a soft, barely audible whirring sound as the gun port in Steele's left hand slid open and the barrel of the dart launcher protruded. Steele raised his arm, his eyes glowing with two red pinpoints as his laser designator switched in, locking on the targets. There were two soft, chuffing sounds as the poison-tipped darts whistled through the air, each one striking dead on. The two men crumpled to the ground without a sound.

"*Damn!*" said Ice.

Steele turned towards him, his eyes still lit up with two small, glowing dots. The effect was unsettling, to say the least. "Still feel like arguing with me?" he said with a smile.

Ice stared at his glowing eyes, then glanced down at the barrel of the dart launcher. About two inches of it protruded from Steele's palm. There was a brief, soft whirring noise and then a click as it retracted, the gun port covered with a sheath of polymer skin slipping back in place.

"What the hell was that?" Ice asked. "What you shoot them with?"

"Poison-tipped darts," said Steele.

"Damn," said Ice. "What other tricks you got up your sleeve?"

"A few," said Steele.

"Like to get me one of those," said Ice, as they trotted towards the door.

"Why don't you ask Higgins?" Steele said. "I'm sure he'd be happy to cut off your arms and legs, take out your brain and see what kind of new gizmos he could install."

"Huh!" said Ice. "Might even be worth it."

Steele glanced at him. "You're a weird man, Ice."

Ice looked down at the bodies. He turned one over with his foot. "Don't know these two," he said. "Akeem bringin' in new blood."

"There might be some friends of yours in there," said Steele.

"If they in there, they ain't no friends of mine," said Ice.

"You sure about that?"

"Don't worry 'bout me, police man," Ice said. "I come here to take care of business, not sing Auld Lang Syne." He unholstered the big .44. "After you."

Steele turned up his hearing slightly and listened for a moment, then went through the door. Ice ducked in behind him, holding the weapon ready.

It was mostly dark inside the warehouse, with only a few lights on, mounted overhead. They stood in an open area, an aisle that ran the entire length of the warehouse. Directly across from them, about fifteen feet away, stood ranks of heavy steel shelving, twenty feet high, row upon row of them, running the length of the building. Steele ran across the open area, into one of the aisles between the shelves. The shelves held mostly wooden crates and steel boxes, stencilled with labels. Steele read one of them.

"Rocket launchers," he said. He glanced at a crate on one of the other shelves. "AR-30 assault rifles," he said. He went down the rows, examining the crates. "Incendiary grenades. .50 caliber machineguns. This must be the stuff Higgins said was hijacked from that Federal ordnance depot. There's enough here to equip a small army. But where the hell's all their security?"

He turned up his hearing. He heard the sound of laughter.

"Yo, man, come on! Don't go takin' all day! Save *me* a piece o' that!"

"Hey, there's lots more left, ain't that right, baby?"

He could hear the sounds of grunting and flesh slapping against flesh. A glass bottle shattered.

Steele's lips turned down in a grimace.

"What is it?" Ice asked.

"Sounds like they're having themselves a party," Steele said. "Come on."

They moved between the rows of crates until they came to another aisle near the center of the warehouse. There were more crates stacked on the other side. They ducked back as someone passed, heading towards the back, a young gang member. As he walked, he zipped his fly.

"Come on, bitch, put some life into it!"

There was the sound of a slap, followed by a girl's grunt. Then, "Eat shit, asshole."

Another slap. Harder this time. Then another.

"Yo, man, take it easy! Don't go gettin' her all bloody!"

"Fuck you! I ain't takin' no lip from this cunt!"

Another slap.

"I know how to shut her up."

"Ain't my kind of party," Ice said, starting forward.

Steele reached out and grabbed him by the shoulder. He pointed up.

There was a glassed-in office area overhead and to their right, accessible by two flights of stairs. Two white men stood at the window, looking down at what was going on below.

"Think you can get up there without being spotted?" Steele said.

"Leave it to me," said Ice.

Moving silently, he headed off down between the aisles. Steele waited. Several moments later, he saw Ice softly tiptoeing up the stairs. The men up in the office were still intent on what was happening below. He unslung his battle rifle and started to move closer. Ice was almost to the top of the stairs. Suddenly the door to the office opened and a man stepped out.

Steele raised his rifle, but Ice lunged forward quickly and seized the man by the throat, lifting him right off his feet. The man's legs jerked as Ice held him up, choking off any sound he might make, then snapped his neck. He carefully laid the body down on the landing and stepped up to the door. He stood outside it for a moment, listening, then opened the door softly and stepped through, ducking down out of sight.

The two men at the open window were still intent on watching the spectacle below. A moment later, Steele saw Ice rise up behind them. A hand went around each of their heads, covering their mouths, and Ice pulled them back away from the window. Perhaps five seconds went by, then Ice appeared at the window, holding his .44. Steele stepped out into the light.

There was a group of about a dozen black men dressed in gang colors standing around an office desk, on which lay the nude body of a young white girl. Her bare legs hung off the desk, and one man stood between them, his pants down around his ankles. Two men stood on either side of the metal desk, holding her arms. Another man stood at the other end, his fly unzipped, forcing himself into the girl's mouth. She struggled, making gagging sounds.

"Get away from her," said Steele, levelling his rifle at them.

The men around the desk spun around, looking at him with startled expressions. The two men brutalizing the girl froze, staring at him slack-jawed. Nobody moved.

"*I said, get away from her!*"

"Yo, man, take it easy! Take it easy! Don't shoot!"

They started looking around, expecting to see other cops. Suddenly, the man who'd been sodomizing the girl screamed in agony. She had bitten down, hard. He smashed his fist down into her face and then a shot reverberated through the warehouse and the top of his skull disintegrated. He collapsed to the floor.

The men glanced up.

"*Ice!*" one of them said.

"You got it," said Ice, aiming his gun down at them. "Now do like the man say. Back off from the girl."

"You son of a bitch! You sold out to the cops!"

"You sold out to Borodini first," said Ice. "Now I said, *back off!*"

Behind him, Steele heard the bolt of an assault rifle being drawn back.

"*Ice, get down!*"

The glass up in the windows shattered and rained down as

bullets sprayed the office. Steele spun around and fired in the
direction of the sound. The gunman hidden behind the crate
flew backwards. The men around the desk broke and scattered in all directions. All save one, who grabbed the unconscious girl and yanked her up, using her as a shield.

"Drop it!" he shouted. "Drop it right now or I'll kill the
bitch!"

He held a knife to her throat.

"Hold it!" Steele shouted.

"Drop it!" shouted the man. "Drop the fuckin' gun!"

Steele dropped the rifle. He held out his left hand.

"Don't," he said. "Don't do it!"

There was a soft whirring sound and then the launcher
fired. The dart whistled through the air and struck the man
right between the eyes. The knife clattered to the floor as the
man fell backwards.

Steele picked up the rifle and ran to the girl. He crouched
over her. She looked dazed. Her face was puffed and bruised
where she'd been struck repeatedly and blood came from her
nose and mouth.

"Ice!"

"I'm okay!" Ice called down from the stairs outside the
office.

Then several assault rifles opened up at once on full
automatic.

Ice vaulted the railing and rolled as he hit the floor. Bullets
slammed into the desk and splintered the crates around him.

Steele picked up the girl and ran, bent over, trying to
shelter her with his body. Ice was right behind him. They
took shelter behind several stacks of heavy wooden crates.
The shooting stopped.

"We in for it now," said Ice. "Should've taken them out
when you had the chance."

"If I opened up on all of them, I might've hit the girl,"
said Steele. "You all right?"

"Thanks to this," said Ice, tapping his body armor where
the bullets had struck his chest. "Bit sore, though."

"Any ribs broken?"

"Don't think so."

Steele glanced at the unconscious, naked girl. "Give he your jacket."

Ice slipped his bullet-riddled jacket off and put it aroun her shoulders. Steele took a quick look at the crates aroun them. None of them was labelled. He drove his fist throug the wood and reached inside. He pulled out a parcel and tore it open. White powder spilled out on the floor. He dipped his finger into it and brought it to his lips.

"Great," he said with a grimace. "An entire warehouse full of weapons and we pick a crate of cocaine to hide behind."

"Least we go out high," said Ice.

"*Ice!*" someone called out. "Ice, you hear me?"

"I hear you!"

"Give us the cop, man! Give us the cop an' we let you go!"

Ice grinned. "You think they mean that?"

"Where's your backup, cop? Where they at, huh?"

Steele handed Ice his rifle. "You know how to use one of these?"

"Squeeze this little trigger, right?"

"Yeah, right," said Steele wryly. "I want you to take her out of here. Get her back to the cab. If they come after you, you and Slim get out of there."

"What about you?"

"Don't worry about me. Just get her out of here, you understand?"

"They be watchin' the doors," said Ice.

"Who needs a door?" asked Steele. He fired several rounds with his .45, then when the answering fire came from the automatic weapons, he went over to the wall behind them, and while the shooting covered the sounds, kicked right through it. Two more kicks and there was an opening wide enough for them to get through. Ice stared at him with amazement. The shooting stopped again.

"Move!" said Steele.

As Ice picked up the unconscious girl and went through the hole in the wall, Steele started moving. He turned his hearing up, listening to the sounds the gunmen made as they moved through the warehouse, toward the spot where they'd been hiding. They had spread out, and as Steele moved, he kept track of their positions, his cybernetic brain instantly pin-pointing their locations from the sounds they made. One of them was about twenty feet to his right, moving toward him. Steele pressed up against one of the heavy metal shelves, waiting for him to get closer. As he came around the corner, Steele reached out with his left hand and plucked the assault rifle out of his grasp, then he drove the butt of it through the man's face, pulverizing it. The man crumpled to the floor without a sound.

Steele checked the rifle's magazine. It had about fifteen rounds left. He bent over, quickly patted down the man's body and found three more magazines. He slipped them into his pockets. Not that he was worried about running out of ammo. The entire warehouse was an arsenal. But that meant, of course, that the opposition had the same advantage. Even more so, because they probably knew where everything was. And though Steele was much harder to kill than an ordinary human being, he knew that he was not invulnerable. A head shot with an armor-piercing bullet fired at high velocity could penetrate his skull casing and damage his brain. The human organs in his chest were vulnerable despite the nysteel ribs and polymer skin, and armor-piercing or high-explosive rounds could penetrate his body armor.

He remembered the crates near the side entrance, the ones that held incendiary grenades. He started to make his way quickly to the other side of the warehouse. With his hearing turned up, he could hear the slightest sounds the others made. He knew exactly where they were, just as if he could see them. They were slowly moving in on the stack of crates containing the cocaine, where Steele and Ice had been hiding moments earlier. They still hadn't realized that Ice and the girl had escaped. And that instead of being the hunters, they were now the hunted.

Moving between the rows of crates, Steele easily avoided the gunmen, slipping around behind them. He found the

crates containing the grenades. With one hand, he pulled one
of the heavy crates out and dumped it on the floor, then
ripped off the nailed-down lid. The noise he made instantly
alerted the gunmen, and he heard them shouting to each other
as they realized that he had slipped around behind them. He
heard them quickly moving his way. He reached into the crate
and started filling his pockets with grenades.

Bullets struck the crates around him. He ducked down and
ran. As Ice had guessed, they had men covering the exits, and
one of those nearest the side door had reached him first.
Steele brought the assault rifle around and fired a burst,
one-handed. The gunman was hurled back by the impact of
the bullets. Steele started moving once again, weaving through
the aisles.

"Back there!" someone shouted.

"You get 'im, Spike? Yo, Spike?"

Steele pulled the pin and lobbed one of the grenades. His
brain instantly computed the trajectory and distance, and his
arm impelled the exact amount of force necessary. The grenade sailed up over the stacks of crates and landed right at
their feet.

"*Jesus—*"

The grenade exploded. A huge blossom of flame lit up the
warehouse as it washed over the crates, igniting them. The
others opened fire. Steele kept moving fast, lobbing the grenades as he ran, dropping them exactly where the gunmen
were. The explosions rocked the building. In moments, the
entire warehouse was in flames. Steele threw the last of the
grenades and ran for the door, firing as he went. The men
guarding the door had fled when the explosions went off.
With all the ordnance in the warehouse, they knew the entire
building would go up like a bomb. He hit the street and kept
on running. Automatic weapons opened up on him, and he
heard the bullets whistling past him. He fired as he ran,
emptying the clip. Without pausing, he slapped in one of his
spares and kept running toward the end of the block. Ice and
Slim were waiting for him. The girl was still unconscious in
the back seat.

"Move!" shouted Steele.

He leaped into the cab, and Slim turned the key in the ignition. The starter motor whined.

"Come on, man!" Ice said.

The starter motor whined again. Suddenly, a howling figure came hurtling out of the darkness and landed on the hood of the cab. Mucus ran from his scarred nose and saliva dribbled from his mouth as he screamed like a wounded beast. His clothes were tattered, with the scrofulous flesh showing through. His entire face and emaciated body were covered with hideous, pustulant sores.

"*Screamer!*" Slim shouted, frantically rolling up his window.

The demented screamer howled and pounded furiously on the windshield. Blood spurted from his knuckles as the windshield cracked.

"Start the damn car!" Ice shouted.

Steele leaned out the window on the driver's side and emptied the magazine of the assault rifle, firing point blank into the screamer. The engine caught as the screamer fell back off the hood of the cab and Slim floored the accelerator. The tires spun and the cab lurched forward, skidding around.

Several figures came running up out of the darkness, backlit by flames from the warehouse. They raised their weapons and started firing at the cab. Steele and Ice leaned out the windows and returned fire as the cab slewed around. Then there was a tremendous explosion as the entire warehouse went up. More explosions followed in rapid succession, shooting huge fireballs up into the night sky. The gunmen on the street were knocked off their feet by the concussive force of the blasts. The cab raced down the cratered street, jolting over potholes, Slim fighting the wheel for control as they headed south toward 125th Street. Behind them, the entire block was in flames.

"*Damn!*" said Ice in an exultant tone as he looked out through the rear windshield. "Man, that's one *fine* sight!"

The girl in the seat beside him stirred, moaning. Steele turned around and looked at her. Her pale face was bruised and puffy. Her lip was cut and there was dried blood on her mouth. Ice had buttoned up the jacket around her. It fit her like a tent. Her long bare legs were splayed out as she slumped in the seat, and her unruly black hair was worn short. She had a long, sharp-featured face with pronounced cheekbones, and she was slim and small breasted. She was perhaps nineteen or twenty years old.

"Anybody have any idea who she is?" Steele asked.

"She goes by the name of Raven," Slim said.

"You know her?" Steele asked.

"Used to be in Rico's stable."

"She's a hooker?"

"Yeah. He tried to sell her to me couple a weeks back. I wasn't buyin'. That little girl one pack o' trouble. Cut up some tricks real bad. Rico must've dumped her on the Skulls, teach her a lesson."

"They taught her, all right," Ice said grimly.

"We'll take her to a hospital," said Steele.

The girl suddenly sat up with a start.

"It's okay, miss," Steele said. "It's over now. You're going to be all right."

She stared at them, a hard, feral expression on her battered face.

"It's okay, we'll take you to a hospital," said Steele.

She suddenly lunged for the door handle.

"Hey, you crazy?" Ice grabbed her and yanked her back, then reached across her and pulled the door closed. "You just sit back an' relax, girl," he said. "Ain't no one gonna hurt you."

She stared at him without a word.

"Man, what a look!" said Ice.

"Take it easy," Steele told her. "You're going to be all right. I'm a police officer. We'll get you some medical attention."

"No," she said. "No hospital."

"You've been hurt," said Steele.

"I've been raped," she said, her lips curling down. "So what? Ain't nothing new."

"We should get you looked at," Steele said.

"I've already been looked at and then some. No. No hospital. You take me there, I ain't gonna stay."

"All right," said Steele. "Where do you want us to take you? Where do you live?"

"Ain't got noplace to live."

"Well, we can't just dump you on the street. What about you, Slim?" Steele asked. "Can she stay with any of your girls?"

"Not me, Jack," Slim said, shaking his head. "I got me enough trouble." He chuckled. "You took her, man, looks like you got her now."

4

"What kind of cop can afford a place like this?" asked Raven, looking around at his penthouse apartment.

"Maybe I'm on the take," said Steele.

"Not if you're going up against Victor Borodini, you're not," she said. "You some kind of fed?"

"Yeah. I'm some kind of fed. Bathroom's through there. You'll probably want to get cleaned up. There's a robe on a hook back of the door, you can use that."

"Thanks."

"At least let me call a doctor to come and have a look at you."

"What for? Nothing's broke. I've been through worse. Lots worse."

"How old are you?"

"How old do you want me to be?"

"Just answer the question."

"I'm twenty-two."

"Really? You look younger."

"Yeah, I know. I tell the johns I am. They like it that way."

"You hungry?"

"No, but I could use a drink. Wash the taste of that bastard's prick out of my mouth."

Steele grimaced at her crudeness. As a cop, he'd met more than his share of Ravens. There were a lot of them around. They were different types and different ages, but they all had several things in common. They talked hard and acted tough

54

and they were cynical beyond belief. They were so accustomed to being used and brutalized that it no longer seemed to matter to them. Sex meant nothing to them. Love? Most of them didn't know the meaning of the word. Their bodies were things somehow separate from themselves, a commodity to be traded in for survival. Many of them had been used and degraded for so long that it was the only thing they understood. It was as if something deep inside of them had died.

Steele understood her all too well. In some respects, cops and hookers had a lot in common. Both lived in worlds where they always saw people at their worst. They had no illusions left about society or the potential cruelty of the human animal.

Twenty-two. His daughter, Cory, was a mere seven years younger. And yet he'd met hookers who were younger still, though in many ways, they were far older than they had any right to be.

He went over to the bar. "What'll you have?"

"Got any Scotch?"

"On the rocks?"

"Neat. In a tall glass."

He poured it.

She shrugged off the jacket Ice had given her, took the drink and headed naked for the bathroom without another word. Steele shook his head and poured himself a drink as well. In the morning, he'd have to see about getting her some clothes. And then what? Then she'd probably go right back on the streets and pick up where she'd left off. She'd find herself another pimp, someone who'd slap her around and treat her like dirt and turn her out to make some money for him. And in a few more years, she'd be all used up, an old woman at twenty-five. What kind of a life was that? And yet, Steele knew that she didn't really think about the future. Girls like Raven rarely did.

They'd tell each other lies about what they'd do when they finally got enough money together to get off the streets, out of "the life," but it never happened. Their money went to their pimps or up their noses or in their veins. After a while, they simply went on automatic pilot. For them, the future was tomorrow, the next hour, the next minute. Survival in tiny doses. If you could call living that way surviving. It occurred to Steele that in some ways, Raven was even more of a machine than he was.

After a while, she came out of the shower, wearing his blue terry robe. Her face was still bruised and puffy from the beating she'd taken, but she'd washed the blood and grime off, and it made for some improvement. She was not unattractive. She was even rather pretty, in a hard and feral sort of way. She went over to the bar and helped herself to the bottle of Scotch. She brought it over to the couch, along with the glass she'd taken to the bathroom, and plopped down. The robe fell away from her legs as she crossed them. They were good legs, long and shapely, and her bare feet were small and incongruously delicate. She wore a small gold ankle bracelet on her right foot.

"Got any smokes?" she said.

"No."

"Shit. I'm dyin' for a cigarette."

Steele picked up the phone and called security. "This is Steele. Anyone down there got any cigarettes? Yeah, cigarettes. Do me a favor and bring some up, will you? Yeah, I appreciate it."

"Thanks," she said. "So your name's Steele, huh?"

"Yeah."

He braced himself for the inevitable questions, but she didn't make the connection. Either that or she hadn't heard of him. Perhaps she didn't watch TV or read the papers. Many of them didn't. They mainlined their entertainment. Steele hadn't noticed any tracks on her arms, but hookers didn't always shoot up in the obvious places. And they didn't always shoot their drugs. She might be a popper or a freak for nose candy. He noticed that she sniffed often, a telltale sign.

"My name's Raven."

"I know. Slim told me."

"How do you know Slim?"

"I don't, really. Ice knows him."

"So that was Ice, huh? Jeez, for a fed, you sure hang around with some strange people. Word is Borodini's got a big contract out on Ice. He workin' for you now?"

"Sort of."

"What's your first name?"

"Donovan."

"Why don't you come over here and sit down, Don?"

"My friends call me Steele," he said. "But we aren't exactly friends. Are we?"

"Doesn't have to be that way," she said.

She recrossed her legs in such a manner that the robe fell away and exposed more of them. They were her best feature and she knew it.

"Come on, sit down. Take a load off. Loosen up and have a drink, honey."

"Don't call me honey. And don't bother coming on to me. I'm not interested. Nothing personal."

"Damaged goods don't turn you on, huh?"

"It isn't that," said Steele.

"Yeah? What, then? I'm not your type or what?"

"I'm just not interested in the sort of relationship that you can buy," said Steele.

"Hey, did I say anything about money?" she said, sounding offended. "You got me out of a bad scene. I just thought maybe I'd show some appreciation, that's all."

"A simple thank you would suffice."

She snorted. "Then what'd you bring me here for?"

"You wouldn't go to the hospital. I didn't know what else to do with you."

The doorbell rang. Steele went over to answer it. It was one of the security guards with a pack of cigarettes and some matches.

"Thanks," said Steele. "How much do I owe you?"

"Forget it, Lieutenant," said the guard. "I'm trying to cut down anyway."

"Appreciate it," Steele said.

"My pleasure, sir."

Steele shut the door and gave the cigarettes to Raven.

"Thanks," she said. She lit one up. "So what's the deal with you and Victor Borodini?" she asked.

"I intend to bring him down."

"Good luck. When he hears about what you did tonight, he'll be comin' after you."

"I'm counting on that."

She gave him an appraising look. "You're either very tough or very stupid," she said. "What you did tonight was crazy. Borodini's gonna make a point of finding out who you are and makin' you pay for it. And your bein' a fed's not gonna bother him one bit."

"I didn't expect it would," said Steele. "Look, I'm going to wash up and go to bed. You can use the spare bedroom over there. Help yourself to the bar. If you feel like watching the idiot box, go right ahead, just don't turn it up too loud. And don't mess around with the other screens. They're computer terminals, and there's nothing there that would interest you. Just make yourself comfortable and stay out of trouble. Don't mess with my things. In the morning, I'll see about getting you some clothes. You gonna be hurting later?"

"I'm no junkie," she said, bristling at the suggestion.

"Tell me the truth," said Steele. "If you're going to start hurting, I'll see what I can do to get you fixed. I don't need an addict going through withdrawal on my hands."

"I do some blow once in a while, but I ain't hooked," she said. She held up the bottle of Scotch. "This'll do me fine."

"Okay," said Steele. "Just behave yourself. I'll see you in the morning."

He wasn't really surprised when he heard his bedroom door open softly in the middle of the night. She stood in the doorway for a moment, listening. He made his breathing sound regular and heavy, as if he were asleep. The door closed softly once again and a short while later, he heard her rummaging around. She was being very quiet, but with his hearing turned up, he could hear everything she did, pinpointing her location as she moved around the apartment. He heard her soft, sharp intake of breath as she opened up the gun cabinet. He got out of bed.

She was bent over the lower drawers, where he kept his ammo, magazines and holster rigs. She didn't hear him come in.

"Find anything you like?" he said.

She got up quickly and spun around. She had put on a set of his black police fatigues and boots. They were large on her and she had tucked the pant legs into the boots and rolled up the sleeves. She had one of his 9 mm.'s held in her right hand and a loaded magazine in the other. She started to insert the magazine into the pistol, but he quickly crossed the room and wrenched it out of her hand as she brought it up. She had tucked one of his commando knives into her waistband and she grabbed for it. He easily caught her wrist as she brought the knife down in a stabbing motion, and, careful not to crush her bones, he squeezed. She gasped with pain, and he took the knife out of her hand.

"That was really stupid," Steele said. "What the hell did you think you were doing?"

"What does it look like?" she asked, gritting her teeth with pain and holding her wrist.

"How did you expect to get past security?" he asked.

"I was gonna tell them that we did our thing and you were sending me away."

"You don't think they would have called me to check?"

"I was gonna tell them you'd gone to sleep and didn't want to be disturbed. And if they didn't buy it, then I had the gun."

"You would've been shot," said Steele. "Those men down there aren't your run-of-the-mill building security. They're trained federal agents. Now put back everything you took, and go to bed."

He handed the gun and the knife back to her.

She stared at him, stunned.

"That's it?" she said with disbelief. "That's all you're gonna do?"

"What you want me to do, slap you around? I don't get my kicks that way. But I'm only going to tell you once. If you give me any more trouble tonight, I'll just break both your arms. Now put the stuff back, and go to bed."

He turned around and went back to his bedroom, leaving her with a knife and a loaded gun in her hands.

She stared at his back as he went through the bedroom door and closed it. Then she carefully put everything back exactly

where she found it, stripped off the clothes she took and went
into the spare bedroom. Steele didn't hear another sound out
of her all night.

Dev Cooper sat up most of the night in his apartment on
Sutton Place, drinking cup after cup of black coffee and
staring at the computer screen. He felt a strange, nervous
excitement, like a little boy doing something he knew he
shouldn't have been doing.

Earlier that day, he'd had lunch with Dr. Phillip Gates, the
project's chief cybernetics engineer, the man in charge of the
team that had programmed Steele's brain. A husky, gruff sort
of man. Gates had at first struck him as being rude and
unfriendly, but Dev soon discovered that the impression was
erroneous. Most people he'd met so far in New York City
struck him that way, and it was merely a result of a different
sort of mindset and rhythm from that which Dev had grown
accustomed to growing up in the southwest.

People in New York simply moved at a much faster pace.
They spoke more quickly and they got right down to business. It was a different tempo from what Dev was used to, it
threw him a bit. Since coming to New York, he'd made an
effort to adjust and blend in more. He had a new wardrobe
now, more in keeping with life in Midtown than his western
clothing was, though he still wore his boots. He wouldn't
have felt comfortable in shoes, and he missed wearing his
Stetson. It was like a part of him, but here in Midtown, it
made him too conspicuous. So he had become something of a
hybrid in his well tailored, three-piece suit and western boots,
learning to match his rhythms to those of the people that he
worked with.

He missed New Mexico, and he missed his comfortable
little house back in White Rock, the small suburb of Santa Fe
where many of the personnel who worked out at the Los
Alamos labs lived. He missed the easy pace out there, the
relaxed and understated lifestyle, the way the women dressed
in Santa Fe, in graceful Spanish skirts and boots, embroidered
blouses, concha belts and Indian jewelry. Compared to them,
the women in New York all looked severe and hard and

considerably less feminine. But most of all, he missed the country.

He missed the red earth of New Mexico, the rolling hills covered with sage, mesquite and the bright, yellow-blooming chamisa. He missed his long walks in Bandolier Canyon, where he could stroll along the wooded riverbanks while hundreds of hermit thrushes fluttered through the branches all around him and hawks and turkey vultures soared on the thermals overhead, scanning the ground below in search of food. He used to spend hours among the pueblo ruins dotting the canyon walls, climbing up into the caves and imagining how the primitive tribes there, descendants of the Anasazi, must have lived hundreds of years ago. The entire canyon was a result of a huge volcanic eruption that had spewed out over fifty cubic miles of volcanic ash, enough, if it were concrete, to pave a road from the Earth to the Sun. He could stand down in that canyon and immerse himself in the tranquility of time.

He had once taken a pack trip by horseback out to Chaco Canyon, on the grounds of what had been the Navajo reservation before the virus had wiped them all out. There, in the middle of one of the most inhospitable areas of the southwestern desert, the Anasazi—the ''Ancient Ones''—had built their cities of meticulously laid sandstone brick held together by mud mortar. It was a harsh, desert country, surrounded by sandstone cliffs. The winters were long, there was little rainfall and the growing seasons were short. Yet the Anasazi had established their culture there in cities that were, in some ways, as complex as New York. In the year 1000, there may have been as many as 5,000 people living in some 400 settlements in Chaco Canyon, in multistory stone villages such as Pueblo Bonito, Chetro Ketl and Hungo Pavi, all tied together by an extensive system of sophisticated roads laid out in straight lines and bordered by masonry walls. Many of the towns were D-shaped, with the interconnected stone buildings running in a semicircle around large central plazas that held large subterranean kivas, circular pits walled with stone, their roofs supported by rubble-filled masonry columns, the walls set with niches meant for sacrificial offerings.

Dev had stood within the ruins of one of the larger kivas, over 45 feet in diameter, and imagined the Ancient Ones holding their religious ceremonies around the vented fires. He felt somehow connected to the spirits of those people, whom the Indians had believed still inhabited the ruins, which still stood after over a thousand years, their exquisite stonework giving evidence of the culture that once thrived there.

To Dev, those ancient ruins were as compelling as those of Greece and Rome. He felt, somehow, that some of his ancestors had once lived there before a prolonged drought in the San Juan Basin drove them out, to scatter throughout the southwest and merge with other tribes. And he wondered now if someday some future archaeologists, perhaps even from another planet, might not puzzle over the ruins of New York City in much the same way he had wondered about the Anasazi ruins, asking themselves who these people were and what had happened to them. What tragedy had befallen them to make them disappear without a trace, leaving behind only the ruins of their architecture to give silent testimony to the greatness they had once achieved?

It had almost happened. The Bio-War and the brief nuclear exchange that had accompanied it had almost brought an end to modern civilization. The population of the world was now a fraction of what it once had been. Cities where the bombs had fallen were in ruins. Radioactive hot spots could be found throughout the country, as well as in Europe and the Soviet Union. We almost did it to ourselves, thought Dev, but now we've got another chance. If only we don't waste it.

The trouble was, it seemed as if humanity had not learned anything from the disaster of the Bio-War. Survival was the number one priority as the ravaged cities struggled to rebuild what they had lost. With the imperative of procreation, many people were now having children in their early teens, future workers to staff the overtaxed factories and farms, to fill out the ranks of the military and police, to help the human race rise up from the ashes of destruction and take up where it left off—headed, it often seemed to Dev, on the same course that had almost brought it to annihilation.

That was why he had jumped at the chance to work on

Project Download. To Dev and many of his former colleagues at Los Alamos, it had seemed like a bright hope for the future. The process of brain/computer interface had the potential for working miracles in human education, and it was in education that the hope for real progress lay. Education that would keep people from making the same mistakes, teach them that they were merely a part of Nature, not the masters of it. Now, more than ever before, ignorance was the enemy. Knowledge could keep them from winding up like the Anasazi, nothing but ghosts inhabiting the ruins of a once-great civilization.

But since he had arrived at project headquarters in New York, Dev had experienced nothing but concern about how that knowledge was being used. The program now running in his personal computer both fascinated and frightened him. And he wondered what Higgins would say if he knew he had it.

As Steele's therapist, Dev Cooper had been frustrated ever since he arrived in New York to take over from the late Dr. Susan Carmody. It was his job to conduct an ongoing evaluation of the state of Steele's cybernetic personality, and he had nothing to go on but his own best instincts. The science of psychocybernetics was in its infancy, and there existed no body of work to guide him. There had never before been a man with a cybernetic brain, and Dev was faced with trying to find his own way, like a blind man groping in the darkness, trying to integrate what he knew of human psychotherapy with the science of cybernetics. And with Steele out working for Higgins much of the time as part of the ongoing project R&D, Dev's time with him was limited.

He had made a point of getting close to Dr. Phillip Gates and Dr. Julie Nakamura and other members of the Project Steele team, especially those who had been involved in the programming of his electronic brain. He pestered them with endless questions, risking their annoyance, desperate to find out as much as he could about his unusual and somewhat recalcitrant patient. He wished he could spend 24 hours a day with Steele and it still would not have been enough. As things stood, there simply wasn't enough time for him to conduct a proper scientific study under such conditions. He had mentioned this to Gates while they were having lunch, voicing his frustration, not really expecting Gates to hand him a solution, but to his surprise, that was exactly what Gates did.

Gates sat there, holding his pipe in his mouth, and he had grunted, which was his way of acknowledging a statement, then he had considered what Dev said not as a simple expression of frustration, but as a problem that he'd been asked to solve. He had thought about it for a moment, then nodded several times and said, "Well, if you need to spend more time with Steele, and Steele is not available as often as you'd like, I could let you have the next best thing. I'll simply run off a backup copy of his program for you."

Dev had stared at him, not certain he had heard correctly.

"A copy of his program?" he had said. "His mental engrams, you mean?"

Gates had shrugged. "Why not? You're his therapist, after all. It's really nothing but software. I don't see why you can't have a copy. All you'd need to do is load it into your PC and conduct your sessions with the program. It would be just the same as having Steele there, since his brain was programmed with the exact same data. The only difference is he won't be there in person, but I don't see where that would matter, really. In fact, it would probably be much more convenient. With the program booted up, you could either enter your questions into your PC or hook up a voice synthesizer peripheral and just talk to it."

"And it would answer? Just like Steele, I mean?" asked Dev, amazed.

"Well, it might not sound like him, but if you really wanted to, I suppose we could program the synthesizer to duplicate his voice. It's no big deal, though I don't see why that would be necessary. If it's just information that you want, what difference does it make what the program sounds like?"

"Well . . . I suppose it could make a difference," Dev had said, still slightly overwhelmed by the idea. "A therapist can often tell a great deal by a patient's speech mannerisms, the inflection of the voice and so on. . . ."

Gates had shrugged. "Okay. So we'll program it to sound like Steele. That's no problem."

"But . . . would it be the same?"

"Why shouldn't it be the same?" Gates asked. "It's Steele's program. I ought to know, I wrote it myself. With some help from the team, of course. The program is essentially his identity. His personality, downloaded from his brain and augmented with some ancillary data. It's the same thing we'd use to reprogram him if anything happened to cause a loss of data, such as an injury to the brain or a glitch of some sort. It's an exact duplicate of the program he's running on right now, so it would respond exactly as he would respond. It should solve your problem. If you like, I could run off a copy for you right now. You can use it in your office or take it with you to work with at home. That way, you wouldn't even need Steele there. In effect, you could boot him up and talk to him anytime you like."

"But . . . would I be allowed to take the program home with me?" asked Dev, still a bit taken aback by Gates' casual attitude about the whole thing. "Higgins said he didn't want classified material leaving the premises."

"They search you when you leave?" said Gates.

"No, but—"

"So who's to know? It's not as if you're going to sell it to some foreign power or something. What would they do with it, in any case? It's just a program, it wouldn't tell them anything about the hardware. Look, don't worry about it. I take home classified material all the time. And most of it's pretty innocuous stuff. Hell, they'd classify the toilet paper in this place if it occurred to them. CIA, you know? You learn to work around them, otherwise you'd never get any damn thing done."

He had gone with Gates back to his office, where Gates pulled the backup copy out of his safe and ran off a copy for him, as casually as a computer hacker sharing protected software with a friend. And it occurred to Dev that Gates, with a typical engineer's mentality, saw things in purely analytical, technical terms. He didn't really think of Steele as anything more than just another A1 program that he "wrote."

In fact, those had been the very words he'd used. Where he himself had been primarily concerned with reinforcing Steele's conception of his own humanity, to Gates, Steele was nothing more than a machine, "hardware," as he had put it, animated only by the software he was programmed with. Never mind that the "software" was actually Steele's human personality, downloaded from his organic brain.

Gates didn't think of it that way. The way he saw it, he had taken some raw data, organized it, debugged it with "ancillary data" and assembled it into the program that animated Steele. That Steele "ran" on, as he had said. To him, it wasn't a human personality that had been transferred into a cybernetic brain, it was a program he had "written," as if he had created it from scratch. He simply didn't think of it in any other way.

Dev had waited in his office as Gates went out and brought back a VS peripheral, and then he'd watched as Gates programmed the synthesizer to respond in Steele's voice, working from the data that he had on file. He made the final adjustments, locked them in, boxed up the peripheral and handed it to Dev, along with a copy of the program.

"Just slip those into your briefcase when you leave tonight," he said with a wink. "They probably won't check, but if they do, just tell them it's a new VS peripheral I checked out for you for your home PC and a test program to make sure it runs okay. They won't know any better, and if they have any questions, just have them check with me. Given your clearance, they probably won't even bother."

And they hadn't. Dev had left the building with the backup copy of Steele's program in his briefcase, half expecting to be stopped, feeling the nervous anxiety of a young boy shoplifting for the first time. But no one had stopped him, and he had hurried home to hook up the VS peripheral and load the program into his home computer, on loan from the project. Once that was done, it took him close to an hour to work up the courage to boot it up. He couldn't shake the feeling that he was doing something wrong. And, technically, he was. He had taken classified data from the project lab without official authorization. For the first time in his life, he had committed a crime. But it wasn't that which bothered him so much as the fact of what he was about to do.

He was about to bring a duplicate of Steele on line in his computer, to interact with an electronic clone of Steele's human personality. It seemed incredible, but certainly no more incredible than the idea of a man with a computer brain. It was almost a foregone conclusion, ever since the first implantable brain electrode had been designed back in the late twentieth century, enabling the first primitive experiments with data and pictures to be transmitted directly to the brain via a tiny chip that interlaced with brain nerve endings. The development of the nanoprocessor followed, one thousand times more powerful than microprocessors, enabling the manufacture of wristband computers that could plug into a keyboard, screen, other peripherals and larger systems. Then the picoprocessor came, one million times more powerful, constructed of molecule-sized circuits, patterned on DNA and grown in a petri dish. The technology was there; the research in brains communicating with computers fully underway when it was interrupted by the war, and Project Download had picked up where they left off. Only the lack of the proper surgical techniques and the accompanying political implications had prevented the implantation of the first artificial brain.

Sophisticated artificial intelligence units with programs capable of duplicating the characteristics of human intelligence already existed at the close of the twentieth century. The only real obstacle to computers truly capable of duplicating human reasoning was not the sophistication of the technology so much as the lack of knowledge concerning human perception, which led AI scientists into the study of cognitive psychology, the beginnings of what was to become the new scientific field of psychocybernetics. No one had doubted that the day would come when the first artificial brain would be implanted in a human being, but in the research of the scientific and technological aspects of the problem, the philosophical aspects of it had received short shrift.

Could a man with a computer for a brain still be considered human, even if the data the artificial brain contained was

transcribed from his own human mental engrams? Could a
machine possess a soul? And if that human data could be
transcribed into software, then would backup copies of that
software become human clones, possessing all the attributes
of humanity except a body made of flesh and blood?

As Dev sat at his computer drinking endless cups of coffee
and almost trembling with anticipation, with anxiety, with
both fear and fascination, he wondered if Phil Gates had fully
realized the implications of what he'd done in giving him a
copy of Steele's program. To Gates, locked into his engineer's mentality, it was no more than software. To Dev
Cooper, it was the essence of a human being that he was
about to boot up on his computer. An electronic clone. A
program with—could it be possible?—a soul. And he could
not escape the feeling that what he was about to do was
wrong, somehow obscene. Nor could he resist it, either. He
felt like Dr. Frankenstein.

It's alive. . . .It's alive. . . .

He felt himself on the threshold of the unknown, of one of
life's great mysteries. How could Gates have so casually
given him the opportunity to do such a momentous thing?
Because, amazingly, he did not consider it as a momentous
thing, but as just another program he could work with. No
more, no less.

Only how would Steele respond if he knew what he was
about to do? Dev didn't dare tell him. If something went
wrong here, he told himself, then it was better that it went
wrong with just a backup copy instead of Steele himself. That
made it safer for his patient. Conducting therapy this way
could revolutionize the science of psychiatry. Therapists would
be able to use brain/computer interface to make copies of
their patients' mental engrams and work with them, free of
the anxiety of making a mistake, able to tell in advance how a
patient would respond to treatment based on how the program
would respond. Only . . .

. . . . if the copy was the same thing as the patient, was it,
in fact, no more than a copy . . . only software . . . or was it
a patient *in itself*, possessing the same human vulnerability as
the brain it was transcribed from? Dev felt himself on the

threshold of a dramatic new step in the field of psychotherapy and, at the same time, on the edge of an abyss.

Gates had no comprehension of what he had done to him. Dev Cooper was afraid. He was afraid to do it. . . . and he was afraid not to.

Dev didn't smoke, but earlier that evening, he had gone out and bought a pack of cigarettes. He would have bought a bottle, too, but he was afraid to take a drink. He needed to be completely sober for this. He swallowed hard and started his tape recorder. Then, after staring at it for a moment, he switched it off again, realizing belatedly that he didn't really need it. He could simply save the session. Jesus, he thought, this really is incredible. He wondered how the program would respond. He wondered what he'd say to it.

Only one way to find out.

He lit up a cigarette, inhaled, coughed, took a deep breath and booted up the program.

A second passed.

A second that seemed like an eternity.

And then Steele's voice came from the speaker.

It said, "Where am I?"

5

Victor Borodini stood at the large bay window in the den of his estate, looking out over Cold Spring Harbor. The harbor was like a long finger of water extending into the north shore of Long Island, bounded on the east by Huntington, with Lloyd Point to the northeast, and on the west by Sagamore Hill and Oyster Bay and Bayville to the northwest. The Borodini estate was located at the southernmost tip of the harbor, on a rise overlooking the water. The settlement known as the Borodini enclave included the towns of Cold Spring Harbor, Huntington, Lloyd Harbor, Halesite, Bayville and Oyster Bay.

At one time, it had been an exclusive residential area, Gatsby country, home to millionaires. As the area became more populated, the upper middle class moved in and it became a wealthy Long Island suburb, though palatial mansions still dotted the north shore. The harbor, once filled with sailboats bobbing at their moorings, was now mined, with no channel markers to indicate where death lurked just beneath the surface of the water. The crews manning the armed patrol boats had memorized the maps that marked the location of the mines, and when they came in to the docks at the edge of the estate, they came in slowly, cruising with an uneasy caution and scanning the water all around them in case any of the mines had drifted loose. A patrol boat and its entire crew had once been lost that way.

Floodlights illuminated the harbor around the back of the estate, the light glinting off the rippling water. The gun emplacements at the foot of the sloping lawn stood like shadowy sentinels in the floodlit night. Borodini turned from the thick, bulletproof glass and faced the men standing behind him. He was dressed in a black silk robe with gold trim and matching black silk pajamas. The letter B was embroidered in fancy gold script over his breast. He had soft black velvet slippers on his feet, and his jet-black hair, graying at the temples, was immaculately combed and styled. His finger-nails were manicured, and he wore a heavy gold signet ring on his right hand, a large diamond on his left. He opened the enamel box on his dark walnut desk, took out a cigarette and lit it with a heavy gold desk lighter. Despite the lateness of the hour, the five men who stood facing him were all fully dressed in suits and ties. They were all silent, attentive, and uneasy.

"How did it happen?" Borodini asked softly, his dark eyes boring into them.

"According to a couple of the Skulls who got away, it was an entire Strike Force assault team. Ice brought them to the warehouse, and they just hit 'em from all sides."

"Did they?"

"Yes, sir."

"Bring them in."

The man who'd spoken nodded to a couple of the others, and they left the room. A moment later, they came back in, escorting two young gang members with them.

"You know who I am?" said Borodini.

"Yes, sir, Mr. Borodini."

"And you know why you're here?"

They looked down at the floor. "We couldn't help it, Mr. Borodini. They had us outnumbered. There musta been twenty, thirty of 'em, hit us all at once. We fought 'em, but there wasn't nuthin' we could do. There was too many of 'em."

"Twenty or thirty," Borodini said.

"That's right. At least."

"And Ice was with them?"

"Yeah. He brought 'em all right to the warehouse."

"So you were outnumbered and outgunned."

"Yeah, that's right."

"In an entire warehouse full of weapons?"

"They just hit us from all sides, Mr. Borodini. There just wasn't no time to do nuthin'."

"I want you to listen to something," Borodini said, staring at them. He reached for his desk and hit the play button on his answering machine.

"This is Ice," the deep voice said, "and I got a message for Victor Borodini. Tell that motherfucker that me and my man Steele had ourselves a party tonight. The two of us done made a bonfire of his warehouse. An' his boys were so busy havin' themselves a gang bang, they never even saw us comin'. Next time, maybe they keep their peckers in their pants and their eyes open. Won't help them none, though. You tell Borodini that contract he put out on me gonna *cost* him. We only gettin' started. Have a nice day."

The tape stopped.

"An entire Strike Force assault team?" said Borodini. "Twenty or thirty men, at least? Isn't that what you said?"

The two gang members avoided his gaze.

Borodini turned away toward the window. "Kill them."

"No, *wait*! Mr. Borodini, *please*. . . ."

The two Skulls were dragged out of the room.

"Tommy . . ."

"Yes, Papa?"

"I want you to take charge of this thing personally," said Borodini. "A thing like this makes me look bad. I want that goddamn cyborg taken out. And the nigger, too. I don't care what it takes, just get it done. I want their fucking heads boxed and delivered to the TV news."

"I'll take care of it, Papa."

"See that you do."

It was a warm, pleasant summer day, and they were playing in the park. Steele's wife was spreading out their picnic lunch on the blanket while their three children, their little girl and the twin boys, played with the dog. Steele glanced over at his wife, and she smiled, brushing her long black hair away from her face. It was a bucolic, peaceful scene, but there was something wrong with it. They never had a dog. And the woman wasn't Janice. Janice was a blonde. And they had two kids, not three. Cory and Jason. They were blond like their mother. These kids all had dark brown hair. And none of them looked like him. He struggled to recall their names as they called out to him, shouting, "Daddy! Daddy! Look! Daddy!"

Who were they?

He turned to their mother. She smiled and blew him a kiss. A name came to him suddenly. *Donna.* Her name was Donna. She was his wife.

But his wife's name was Janice.

"Daddy! Daddy!"

He had no idea who they were. Suddenly, a horrible scream broke the stillness of the park. In an instant, it was night.

"*My children! My children!*" Donna screamed.

His mother had suddenly appeared from out of nowhere, her clothing torn and filthy, her face covered with the hideous, running sores of a screamer. Just as in his childhood, when she had come bursting through the door of their apartment, mindless with the awful virus raging in her system, she descended on the children as she had attacked his two younger brothers, clasping them to her chest and biting at them like a rabid dog. He stood rooted to the spot, unable to move as he heard their agonized screaming.

"*Daddeeeee!*"

He came awake with a cry. Raven was sitting on the edge of his bed, naked, her hands on his shoulders.

"It's okay, it's okay," she said, "it was just a dream."

He stared at her wildly, breathing hard.

"You had a nightmare," she said. "I heard you next door. It must've been a bad one, huh?"

Steele shut his eyes briefly and took a ragged breath. "Yeah. It was a bad one."

"Well, it's okay now," she said, putting her arms around him and pulling him close. "It's okay. It's okay."

She slipped beneath the covers and lay down next to him, holding him in her arms.

"I'll stay right here," she said softly, stroking his hair lightly. "It'll be all right. Just go to sleep now. No more bad dreams."

He lay with his head pillowed on her breasts while she gently stroked his hair. After a while, he fell asleep. And there were no more dreams.

He awoke to the smell of fresh coffee. He got dressed and went out into the kitchen. Raven stood by the stove, barefoot, in his bathrobe, cooking up some eggs and bacon. He glanced at the clock. It was ten.

"I overslept," he said.

"You had a bad night," she said. "You didn't have hardly anything in your refrigerator, so I went down and asked one of the guards to go pick up a few things. I told him that you'd pay him back. He said not to worry about it."

"You went down to the lobby like that?" said Steele.

She shrugged. "I didn't know the number to call down. Oh, and you had a phone call. I picked it up quick so it wouldn't wake you. Somebody named Higgins. Wanted to know who the hell I was, then he wanted me to wake you. I told him to go fuck himself, you'd call him back when you got up."

Steele grinned. "How did he take that?"

"Who knows? I hung up. I hope you like your eggs scrambled. That's the only way I know how to make 'em."

He thought about telling her that he usually didn't eat breakfast, but instead he said, "Scrambled will be fine."

"I made some fresh coffee. I don't know how you take it, but there's some milk in the fridge."

"I take it black. Thanks."

He poured himself a cup.

"You're very domestic this morning," he said.

She shrugged. "Hey, hookers gotta eat too, you know."

"That was nice, what you did last night."

She shrugged again. "I get bad dreams too. All the time. It's a drag when you're alone." She paused. "I put all the stuff back, just like you said."

"Good."

"I guess it was a pretty shitty thing to do. Trying to rip you off, I mean."

"So why'd you do it?"

"I don't know. I guess you either rip people off or you get ripped off, know what I mean?"

"I suppose that's one attitude to take. But there are others."

"Would you have really broken my arms?"

"Probably, if you tried it again."

"Yeah. That's what I figured. You don't seem like the type who'd just make threats." She dumped the eggs and bacon on two plates and brought them over to the table. "Toast'll be ready in a minute."

She lit up a cigarette.

"I would've shot you, you know. When you walked in on me."

"I don't doubt it," Steele said, taking a mouthful of eggs.

"Doesn't that bother you?"

"I've been shot before."

She gave a brief, snorting laugh and shook her head. "I can't figure you out."

"Why bother trying?"

She shook her head. "I don't know. There's just something. . . . different about you."

"Yeah?"

"Yeah. I can't put my finger on it. It's like last night, when you took the gun away from me, and then I pulled the knife, and you took that away, too, and then you didn't *do* anything. I mean, yeah, you told me if I got out of line again, you'd break my arms, but then you gave the gun and the knife back to me and told me to put all the stuff back and, like, you just turned your back and walked away. I could've shot you or tried to stab you, but it's like you knew I wouldn't. I mean, you just *knew*. Now if it was Rico—he was my pimp—he would've trashed me just to show me who was boss, to prove how strong he was, but you didn't even have to do that. You didn't even have to lay a finger on me, and I knew not to mess with you. I mean, Rico would *never* turn his back on me. And then later on, when you had that dream, and I got into bed with you and you were holding me. . . . you were scared. And you weren't afraid to let me see that.''

"Everyone gets scared at one time or another," said Steele.

"Yeah, but most people are afraid to show it. Because if you show someone you're afraid, it's like showing them a weakness.''

"Fear isn't a weakness," Steele said. "Being afraid to admit you feel it is a weakness."

"It takes being strong to say that.''

"No," said Steele. "It just takes being honest.''

She gazed at him for a moment, then looked away. "Your eggs okay? I ain't much of a cook.''

"They're fine. I just don't usually eat breakfast.''

"Yeah? Me, neither. Cup of coffee and a cigarette's about all I can handle in the morning. But this morning, I was hungry. So who's this Higgins guy?''

"He's the man who pays the rent on this place,'' Steele said.

"Oh," she said. "He's the guy you work for, huh? I guess I shouldn't have hung up on him.''

"Don't worry about it. I've done it myself. I've got a feeling I know what he wanted anyway. It was probably about our blowing up Borodini's warehouse full of stolen ordnance last night. I have a feeling he would have been lots happier if I'd just called in a strike and recaptured all the hardware.''

"So why didn't you?''

"Because I didn't care about the ordnance. I wanted to rub Borodini's nose in it. I wanted him to know that it was me and Ice who did it and cost him all that money. Word will get around, and it will make him look bad.''

"Won't that get you in trouble with your boss?''

"Higgins told me to recover the ordnance if I could and to destroy it if I couldn't. Well, for all I know, by the time I called in for backup and they got there, Borodini could have had his people move the stuff, so I destroyed it, just like the man said.''

She grinned. "You do things pretty much your own way, don't you?''

"That way, I can be sure that they get done," said Steele.

The doorbell rang and Steele went to answer it. It was Ice. He wore dark slacks and a black tee-shirt with his gold chain around his neck. His huge muscles bulged against the shirt so that it looked like it was painted on. And, as usual, he wore his shades.

"You catch the news this mornin'?" he said.

"No, I slept late."

Ice glanced at Raven in Steele's bathrobe. He grinned. "Uh-huh."

"It's not what you think," said Steele.

"Hey, ain't none of my business," Ice replied. "But they had a nice shot of that bonfire we had us last night. Got a chopper out there not long after we left. You shoulda seen it. Whole damn block went up. Done mentioned our names, too."

Steele frowned. "How'd they find out so fast?"

"I done called 'em," Ice said. "Right after we got in last night. Told 'em what was in that warehouse, who it belonged to, and what we did to it. And then I called the man himself."

"You called Borodini?"

"Left the man a message. Gave him our warmest regards. *Hah*!"

"You two are crazy," Raven said, shaking her head. "You don't know who you're dealing with."

"You got that wrong, sister. Man don't know who *he* dealin' with," said Ice. "So what's on the agenda for today, police man?"

"I've got to go see Higgins," Steele said. "Meanwhile, why don't you take Raven out and buy her some clothes?"

"You want me to go *shoppin'*?" Ice said. "With her lookin' like that? What she gonna wear?"

"I'll let her borrow some of my clothes," Steele said. He glanced at Raven and smiled. "They'll be a little big on her, but I think she can manage to fit into 'em. Get her anything she wants."

"Who pickin' up the tab?"

"Charge it to Higgins," Steele said. "Just flash that little government ID he gave you, and have them send the bill to the Federal Building.''

"Yeah? Might pick me up a thing or two while I be at it.''

"Be my guest. I'll meet you back here later.'' He turned to Raven. "You can go borrow some of my fatigues. Just give them back to Ice when you're done with them. Chances are I won't be seeing you again, so take care of yourself, and try to stay out of trouble.''

"You sending me away?'' she said.

Steele glanced at her with surprise. "You didn't expect to stay here, surely?''

"Why not?'' she said. "There's plenty of room. I wouldn't be a bother. I'd behave myself, I promise.''

"Lady seem to like it here,'' said Ice with a smile.

"Look,'' said Steele, "nothing personal, but—''

"Don't send me away,'' she said. "Please. Look, I could help you guys. I know a lot about the Borodini family.''

Steele gave her a wry look. "Now how would you know anything about the Borodinis that would be of any use to us?''

"I used to be Tommy Borodini's girl,'' she said.

"You lyin','' Ice said.

"I ain't lyin','' she said, bristling. "It's the truth.''

You expect me to believe that?'' Steele said.

"I can prove it,'' she said.

She bent down and removed the small gold bracelet from around her ankle. She tossed it on the table in front of Steele. He picked it up and looked at it. It was a delicate ankle ID in 24 karat gold. The little oval nameplate was engraved in fancy script.

"Tommy B,'' read Steele.

"Could be on the level,'' Ice said. "Borodini's son go by the handle Tommy B.''

"You could have got this anywhere,'' said Steele dubiously, though he was looking at her with new interest.

"Yeah, but I didn't,'' she said. "Tommy gave it to me. And there's been pictures took of us together for the papers. If you don't believe me, you could check on that, couldn't you?''

Steele pursed his lips thoughtfully. "Yes, it would be easy enough to check. How long ago would this have been?"

"Five, six years ago. Around six, I think."

Steele frowned. "You would've been about sixteen."

"Yeah. That's about right. I started seein' Tommy when I was fifteen."

"*Fifteen*?" said Steele. "Tommy Borodini would have been about twenty-eight, twenty-nine."

"Yeah, that's right," she said.

"Tommy always did like 'em on the young side," Ice said wryly.

"How'd you wind up on the streets?" asked Steele.

"I caught Tommy fuckin' off on me with one of my girl-friends when I was seventeen," she said. "Walked in on 'em together. He laughed and wanted me to join the party. I grabbed a knife and cut him."

"Where?" asked Ice.

"On his face," she said. "Right here." She traced a line on her cheek.

Ice nodded. "Tommy B's got himself a scar on his right cheek," he told Steele.

"Bastard trashed me," Raven said. "Beat on me till I couldn't even crawl. Then he gave me to some of his boys, and after they were through havin' their fun, he had them throw me in a car and take me to Rico. He turned me out, and I've been with him ever since."

"Why didn't you run away?" asked Steele.

"Don't think I didn't try," she said bitterly. "It ain't so easy. Besides, where was I gonna go? I ain't got no family." She picked up the ankle bracelet. "I kept this—to remind me of what that bastard did. I swore I'd get even with him someday. This could be my chance, Steele. Don't send me away. Please. I got nowhere to go."

Steele glanced at Ice, then looked back at her. "Okay. We'll talk about this later," he said. "Meanwhile, we'd better get you some clothes to wear."

"I need to check the newspaper morgues, about five or six years ago," Steele said to Gates. "Can we get access?"

"Shouldn't be a problem," Gates said. "I can access their microfiche files from here once I get them on line and have them load the right ones. Which paper?"

"Let's try the *Daily News*."

"Okay. What date?"

"I'm not sure. I need to start looking from about six years back."

"What are you looking for?" asked Gates as he started typing in commands.

"A photograph, but I don't know which paper it appeared in or exactly when. I'll have to interface and scan."

"Okay. I'll just set you up for a download via broadcast link. Make yourself comfortable. It'll only take a couple of minutes."

Steele took a seat, and a few moments later, Gates had access to the data.

"Okay. Should only take a second or two to interface you. Hold on."

Steele waited.

"Okay. You're all set."

Steele leaned back and closed his eyes.

An image appeared in his mind, as clearly as if he were looking at it. It was the front page of a newspaper dated six years ago. He locked Raven's image in his mind so that his cybernetic brain would flag it if it came up, then proceeded to scan the files. The images started to come faster and faster, much faster than the ordinary human eye could follow, but he wasn't looking at them with his eyes. His computer brain was sorting through them, seeking the right one. The data kept coming in a blur, months' worth of papers scanned in a matter of seconds, faster and faster, and then . . . bingo! There it was. Fifth day of August, five years earlier, middle of the fourth page. Tommy Borodini leaving a chic Midtown nightspot with a young brunette on his arm. It was undeniably Raven. She had told the truth.

"You find what you're looking for?" said Gates.

"Yeah. You can disconnect."

The image flicked out, and Steele opened his eyes.

"I need some information, but I haven't got the time to

hunt it down now. Could you put together a file for me to take on download?''

"Sure. What do you need?''

"Everything I can get on the Borodini family and their enclave in Cold Spring Harbor. Government and police files, newspaper accounts, the works. Whatever you can get.''

"That could take a while.''

"How long?''

Gates shrugged. "A few hours, maybe more. I could have it for you by this afternoon.''

"Okay. Let me know when you've got it all assembled.''

"No problem.''

"Thanks. I'll check back with you later.'' He left the lab and took the elevator upstairs to Higgins' office. The secretary glanced up as he came in.

"Hello, Nancy. Boss in?''

She nodded. "He's been wanting to see you. He's not in a good mood.''

Steele grimaced. "When is he ever?''

"You've got a point there,'' she said with a smile. "Go right in.''

Higgins was on the phone when he came in. He glanced up, said, "I'll call you back,'' and hung up.

"You wanted to see me?'' Steele said.

"Yeah, about several hours ago,'' said Higgins dryly. "What was with that stunt last night?''

"You told me you wanted to disrupt Borodini's operations in the city,'' Steele said. "Well, I disrupted them.''

"Why the hell didn't you call in for a backup? We could have hit that warehouse and recovered all the ordnance. You didn't have to blow it up, for God's sake!''

"You told me you wanted the stolen ordnance either recovered or destroyed, so I destroyed it.''

"You have any idea how much all that stuff was worth?''

"Along with all the dope in there, it was probably worth a bundle,'' Steele said. "But by the time I called in an assault unit and they got there, they could've moved a lot of it. The moment the Strike Force unit crossed over into no-man's-land, Borodini's people would have been alerted. They would've brought in reinforcements from the gangs, and there would've been a firefight. I didn't want to take that chance. Besides, this way we got some dramatic coverage, and now everybody knows that Borodini got hit by the same two people he put out contracts on. I figure it's a little more embarrassing for him this way.''

"It would have been less embarrassing for me if we could have recovered all that ordnance," said Higgins sourly. "Who's that girl? Security told me you and Ice brought her in last night, wearing nothing but a sportcoat. What you do on your own time is your business, but I don't need some little twit telling me where to get off and then hanging up on me. What's going on?''

"Her name is Raven," Steele said. "She's a hooker."

Higgins grimaced. "Didn't think you went in for that sort of thing.''

"I don't," said Steele. "She was at the warehouse. The Skulls were brutalizing her. Ice and I pulled her out of there. She refused to go to the hospital, and I couldn't very well just turn her loose on the streets like that. Besides, she's got some information that could be very useful.''

"What sort of information?"

"She used to be Tommy Borodini's girl," said Steele. "She caught him cheating on her and they had a fight. She cut his face and he worked her over, then gave her to his boys, after which he had her turned over to a pimp in no-man's-land named Rico. He turned her out and she's been in his stable ever since, but she caused him trouble, so he gave her to the Skulls to teach her a lesson. For obvious reasons, she'd like to get back at Tommy B, so she's offered to help. She was with him for several years. She knows the enclave, and she knows a lot about what goes on in there.''

"That could be useful," Higgins said. "I'll run a make on her. What's her last name?''

"I don't know. She didn't tell me. I don't even know if Raven is her real name, but she was photographed with Tommy B. And she's got a gold ankle bracelet that he gave her with his name on it.''

"Where is she now? Still at your place?"

"She's with Ice," said Steele. "I sent him out to pick up some clothes for her. I couldn't have her running around wearing nothing but my bathrobe."

"I take it I'm going to get the bill?" said Higgins wryly.

"I figure the company can afford it," Steele said.

"You've been doing an awful lot of figuring without checking with me," said Higgins.

"You want me to check with you every time something comes up?"

Higgins sighed. "All right," he said. "But it would be nice if you could keep me posted. If you've got time to call the TV news, you've got time to call me."

"That was Ice," said Steele. "I was busy."

"I'll bet," said Higgins. "That TV reporter's been calling me all day, wanting some sort of statement about what happened last night. The one who did that story on you, Linda Tellerman. She'd like an interview."

"I already told you how I feel about that."

"I don't want to antagonize the media, Steele. They can be a help to us. Good PR can help us with our funding."

"Fine. So you talk to her."

"She wants you," said Higgins, trying to keep his patience. "I understand how you feel, but it wouldn't hurt you to play ball a little. And if you want to get Victor Borodini's goat, a TV interview would be the perfect vehicle."

"Okay, I'll think about it."

"You do that. Dr. Cooper wants to see you before you leave. Stop by his office on your way out."

Dev Cooper looked tired. There were bags under his eyes, and he had neglected to shave that morning. He was looking over some files when Steele came into his office.

"You wanted to see me?"

"Steele. Sit down. How're you doin'?"

"I'm okay. You look worn out, though."

"Didn't get much sleep last night," said Dev with a faint smile. "Got lots of catchin' up to do. Been lookin' over Dr. Carmody's files on you."

"Anything wrong?"

"No, not really. I just wanted to check in with you and see how things were going."

"Okay, I guess," said Steele. "There's no bugs in the program so far as I can tell."

He thought about the dream he'd had last night. He didn't want to tell Cooper about it. It was the same dream he'd had before, only this time, there'd been a new wrinkle. The first time, they'd just been playing in the park, that strange woman who was his wife and yet not his wife and those three children who were his and yet not his. Last night, he'd gotten a name for the woman. Donna. Donna what? He didn't know. And his mother had been in it, too. His real mother, who had contracted Virus 3 and become a screamer. He would never forget the way she'd looked when she came bursting through the door of their apartment, screaming, "My children! My children!"

She had torn her clothes, and her face was already ravaged with the awful running sores. Her face was devoid of any sanity. It was the face of a monster. He had stood rooted to the spot in terror as she had hurled herself upon his two younger brothers, hugging them to her breast and covering them with bloody kisses, and then suddenly she started biting them. His father had not been able to get to her in time to stop her. They struggled and he shot her, but during their struggle, he had become infected. To save Steele's brothers from a fate worse than death, he had shot them both and then turned the gun on himself. The memory of that terrible night had been seared into Steele's consciousness forever.

He didn't know how to account for that dream he had last night. After losing his family that way, he'd had nightmares about that night for years until they finally went away, but last night, the vision came back to haunt him once again. Only it was as if part of the memory was his . . . . and part was someone else's. He had no idea who those children were, but they had called him "Daddy," and he felt, inexplicably, that they were his. And Donna. Who was she? His wife, according to his dream, yet he had never seen her before. And at the same time, he felt as if she *was* his wife. And that was crazy. His wife's name was Janice, and she had divorced him, taking Cory and Jason with her. So who was this stranger who was somehow not a stranger?

Dev Cooper was watching him with a slight frown on his face, but Steele did not want to tell him about the dream. Perhaps he should, but what if it wasn't some sort of peculiar quirk of his normal subconscious mental engrams? What if it was some sort of glitch in the program? They'd put him on downtime once again, and while he was out, Gates and his people would debug him, go through his program with a fine-tooth comb in their search for any glitches. And if they found one, they would take it out. Erase it. Only what *else* would they erase? From his long conversations with Susan Carmody, Steele knew how delicate his mental engrams were. The subconscious, translated into a computer program, was like an incredibly intricate web. . . . touch one strand and all the others quiver. Break one. . . .

"What is it?" Dev asked.

"Nothing," Steele lied. "Just thinking about something I've got to do. I've got some people waiting for me. In fact, I really should be going."

"We haven't had much chance to talk," said Dev.

"We'll do it some other time," said Steele. "Soon. I promise."

He got up to leave.

"Steele?"

He paused uneasily.

"Is there something you're not telling me?"

He forced a smile. "No, I've just got a lot on my mind right now, that's all. Don't worry, Dev. I'm fine. Really."

"You're sure? If there's something bothering you, we really ought to talk about it."

"It's just police business, that's all," said Steele. "I have to go talk to an informer. Might give me a line on Victor Borodini. Soon as I get that all wrapped up, we'll talk. I've really got to go."

"Take care of yourself," said Dev, watching him with a concerned expression on his face.

"Will do. Be seeing you."

Dev sat still for a long moment after he left, then he picked up the phone.

"This is Dr. Cooper," he said. "Let me talk to Dr. Gates."

6

The police cruiser dropped Steele off at the front entrance of his building and started to pull away, but before he could go in, he was intercepted by Linda Tellerman, who came running out of a car parked several yards away.

"Lt. Steele! Wait!"

He resisted an impulse to dash into the lobby and stopped. And as a result, the shots missed him. The high-explosive rounds slammed into the lobby door and blew out the thick glass.

"*Get down!*" he shouted as he dropped to the ground and rolled.

A veteran of covering street battles between gangs and the police, she immediately dropped down to the sidewalk and started scrambling back on her belly for the shelter of her car. The unseen gunman fired again, on full auto, and Steele was forced to scramble away from the entrance as the rounds exploded all around him, which was precisely the gunman's intention, to force him away from shelter and out into the open. The officer who'd dropped him off was halfway down the block, and as the building security guards responded to the shots, he spun the patrol unit around, racing back to cover Steele. He jumped the curb and pulled in close to Steele, interposing the armored vehicle between Steele and the gunman. He threw open the driver's side door and slid over, allowing Steele to enter. He was already calling in for backup.

But Steele didn't get inside. Not yet. Using the car for shelter, he quickly scanned the buildings across the way, following the report of the rifle's shots. He zoomed in on tight focus and spotted the gunman just as he was moving back from the edge of the roof. He leaped into the driver's seat and spun the vehicle around, speeding toward the building's entrance. He jumped the curb, and even before the officer could complete his call, he was already out and running inside the building, shouting back over his shoulder to the officer, "Stay here! Have security cover the entrance! Nobody gets out!"

If the gunman ditched his weapon and came down in the elevator, the officers would stop him. Steele went right for the stairs, taking them three at a time at top speed, his legs churning as he hurtled up the stairs faster than any normal man could run, heading for the roof. He made it in a matter of moments. The gunport slid back in his right hand as the pistol barrel came out. He stood just inside the open door a moment, his hearing turned up, listening for the slightest sound, then he dove out through the doorway and rolled.

No one shot at him. He came up quickly, scanning the rooftop all around him, but there was no sign of the gunman. And then his ears picked up the telltale sounds of boots on metal.

He ran over to the edge of the roof. The gunman was already more than halfway down the fire escape, the rifle slung across his back. Even with his superior speed, Steele knew he wouldn't catch the man before he hit the street. He looked down and saw Linda Tellerman hurrying across the street with her cameraman behind her. The fool woman stopped on the sidewalk right between the two buildings and started setting up, so her cameraman could cover the building entrance where the patrol unit was parked. He saw her turn to the camera, holding her mike. The gunman couldn't fail to see her. He'd be on the ground in seconds, and he'd be able to get to her and use her as a hostage before the men covering the front of the building realized what was going on.

"*Linda!*" Steele shouted at the top of his lungs. "*Get back!*"

She heard him and looked up, then, incredulously, Steele saw her turn to her cameraman and point up at him. As the man trained his camera on Steele, standing at the roof's edge, she stood right where she was and started her "on-the-scene" report.

"Jesus. . . ." Steele said. He looked down. The gunman was almost to the street level. Even with his computer-controlled accuracy, Steele couldn't be certain that a shot wouldn't be deflected by the fire escape. And if he waited till the gunman hit the street. . . . He couldn't take that chance.

He retracted his gun, looked down and took a deep breath.

"*Shit*," he said through gritted teeth.

And dropped right over the side.

He fell straight down, flailing his arms in an effort to keep his body from turning, praying that his fall would be straight and not angle out away from the fire escape. The wind rushed by him as he fell past the astonished gunman, then he lunged out and grabbed the railing of the fire escape, clamping his nysteel fingers around it with all his might. He grunted as his body slammed against the side of the fire escape with tremendous force, making it shudder with the impact, but he managed to retain his grip, and his nysteel shoulder joints held. He pulled himself up and over onto the iron-railed landing. The gunman just above him had recovered from his shock and was quickly unslinging his rifle. Steele raced up the steps toward him.

The gunman brought the rifle up.

Steele raised his right arm, gun barrel sliding out of the port in his hand. He fired.

The 10 mm. bullet struck the rifle, knocking it out of the gunman's grasp.

Then Steele was on him. He knocked the gunman down, then picked him up by the ankles and swung him out over the side, holding him suspended three floors up, head down.

The gunman cried out in fear.

"Who hired you?"

"Don't!" shouted the gunman. "Don't drop me! *Please*!"

Steele let go with one hand.

The gunman screamed in terror as Steele held him upside down with one hand.

"*No! For God's sake! Don't. . . .*"

"Who hired you?"

"*All right, all right! I'll talk! Just don't drop me, please, God. . . .*"

"Was it Borodini?"

"*Yes! Yes! It was Tommy B! Please! Please! Don't let go, Jesus God, please. . . .*"

Steele hauled him back up onto the fire escape. The man collapsed to the landing. "*Jesus Christ!*" he gasped. "*You ain't fuckin' human!*"

Steele reached down and hauled him up to his feet by his shirtfront. He quickly patted him down and relieved him of a pistol fastened down in a shoulder holster inside his jacket and a switchblade knife inside his pants pocket. The man had no other weapons.

The men covering the front entrance had seen where Linda Tellerman had trained her camera and had rushed around to the side of the building. They stood at the bottom of the fire escape with their weapons out.

"*Go ahead and send him down, Lieutenant! We've got him covered!*"

"Get down there before I change my mind and throw you over," Steele said to the gunman.

The man wasted no time scrambling down to the waiting officers. As he got off the fire escape, the police backup units came screeching up. Linda Tellerman was down there with her cameraman, filming the whole thing. Another freak show for the evening news. Steele turned away and leaned back against the stairs of the fire escape, looking up at the roof. He exhaled heavily.

"Jesus, I can't believe I did that," he said to himself.

If he'd missed. . . . His stomach churned and he fought down the rising bile. As he climbed down, Linda Tellerman and her cameraman were filming the gunman being cuffed and taken away, then she came rushing over to him.

"That was really stupid," Steele said to her before she could start talking. "You could've gotten yourself killed."

She waved to the cameraman behind her to stop taping,

then she turned to him and grinned. "I'm not the one who jumped off an eighteen-storey building," she said. "That was the most amazing thing I've ever seen in my entire life! And we've got it all on tape! It'll be incredible!"

"Is that all you care about?"

"It's my job, Steele. And when the people of this city see what you've just done, you'll be a hero. Every kid in Midtown's going to worship you!"

"Yeah? And what happens when some kid jumps off a roof because he saw me do it on TV?" Steele asked. "You gonna film the wet mess on the sidewalk and his mother screaming with grief? You going to stick a mike in her face and ask her how she feels about what happened?"

"Why don't you like me, Steele?"

"For the same reason I don't like all reporters," Steele said. "All you're interested in is sensationalism. You don't really give a damn about people, about their feelings."

"That's not true," she said.

"Isn't it?"

"If you gave me half a chance, I'd try to prove it to you."

"Like the last time, when you told me you weren't taping but you recorded what I said just the same?"

"Okay, you're right, I'm sorry about that. Like it or not, Steele, you're news. But I tried to report that story the way I thought you would have wanted me to. Not in a sensational manner, but in *human* terms."

"Yeah, I especially liked the way you misted up on camera when you said I told you I just didn't want to be a freak show," Steele said wryly. "I thought that was very effective. You should've been an actress, Miss Tellerman."

"What makes you think I was acting?" she asked softly. She turned to her cameraman. "Come on," she said. "Let's get back to the studio."

"Wait," said Steele.

She turned.

"Okay. Go ahead and roll your tape," he said to the cameraman.

The cameraman glanced at her, then raised his minicam. She looked at Steele questioningly, then raised her microphone.

When Ice and Raven returned from their shopping excursion, they saw the damage to the lobby door and immediately guessed what must have happened. The security guards confirmed their suspicions, but reassured them that Steele was all right and that the hitman had been apprehended.

Raven looked very different with clothes on. Before, wrapped in Ice's jacket and later in Steele's bathrobe, she had looked like a lost waif, a vulnerable little girl, albeit with a hard edge to her. Now, she looked a lot less vulnerable. Her face still bore the evidence of her beating, but she had hidden most of it with skillfully applied makeup. She'd had her hair styled and her nails done, and she came in wearing a slinky, close-fitting, black knit dress with a short skirt, stockings and black high-heeled pumps that accented the natural beauty of her legs. The outfit brought out her trashy sexuality.

"The guards told us what happened," she said to Steele when they got upstairs. She looked concerned. "Are you all right?"

"Yeah, I'm okay. You look nice," he said.

"You like it?" she said, doing a model's pirouette for him. "Ice helped me pick it out. You think it's sexy?"

"It is that," said Steele. Ice came in loaded down with boxes of clothing. "What'd you do, buy out the whole store?"

"We just picked up a few things," she said, slightly defensive. "It's okay, isn't it?"

"Yeah, I guess it's okay."

"Look like you had some trouble," Ice said.

Steele nodded. "Tommy B hired himself a hitman. Took some shots at me from the roof across the street."

"I told you they'd come after you," Raven said. "And they're not gonna stop. The Borodinis have a lot of soldiers. They'll just keep after you until they get you."

"Then we'll just have to get them first," said Steele. He turned to Ice. "I've got Gates putting together a complete file on the Borodini enclave," he said. "He should have it ready for me sometime this evening, then we'll see what we can do about putting together a plan of action.''

"You're gonna try to hit the *enclave*?'' Raven said. "That's crazy.''

"Maybe,'' Steele said, "which is why they won't be expecting us to try it.''

"You'll never get inside,'' she said. "That place is like a fortress.''

"Which is why we'll need your help,'' said Steele. "I need you to tell me everything you know about the Borodini enclave and what goes on in there.''

"So does that mean I can stay? You're gonna let me help?''

"Yeah,'' said Steele. "You can stay.''

"I'm standing here with Lt. Donovan Steele,'' said Linda Tellerman, "who, as you just saw, dramatically foiled an attempt against his life moments ago outside his building on Park Avenue. Lt. Steele, do you have any idea who was behind this assassination attempt?''

"Yes, I know exactly who was behind it. The man confessed to me that he was hired to kill me by Tommy Borodini.''

"Victor Borodini's son?''

"That's correct.''

"Do you think this had anything to do with what happened last night, when you destroyed that warehouse allegedly belonging to Victor Borodini?'' she said.

"There's nothing alleged about it,'' Steele said. "That warehouse was full of ordnance stolen from a federal armory. It was also full of drugs meant for the streets of no-man's-land and Midtown. The contraband was being guarded by Victor Borodini's men, along with members of the Skulls street gang, who work for Borodini.''

"The station received a call last night tipping us off to what happened at that warehouse,'' Linda said. "The caller identified himself as Ice. Is that the same man who's the leader of the Skulls?''

"Correct,'' said Steele. "Only Ice was ousted from his position as leader of the Skulls because he refused to take orders from Victor Borodini. As a result, Borodini put out a contract on him. Ice is now cooperating with the authorities to help bring Victor Borodini to justice.''

''So he was the one who tipped you off about that warehouse?''

''That's correct. When we arrived, we found the stolen arms and the drugs. We also found a rape in progress. The Skulls were brutalizing a young woman while Borodini's people watched. Under the circumstances, there was no time to call in for backup. We had to move in fast. They resisted arrest, and in the ensuing gun battle, the warehouse caught fire and was destroyed, but we did manage to get the young woman out. For obvious reasons, her identity's being protected.''

''So you think the attempt against your life today was a direct result of that?''

''I have no doubt of it. Victor Borodini takes a dim view of anything that cuts into his profits. I have it on very good authority that he's put a contract out on me. Word on the streets is that I'm worth half a million dollars to him dead.''

''Doesn't that frighten you?'' she said.

''No, it doesn't frighten me,'' said Steele. ''I'm not afraid of maggots. And in case Victor Borodini's watching, I'd like to tell him that the authorities are fed up with two-bit crime lords who try to pose as legitimate businessmen and libertarians while they work behind the scenes against the people of this city, using the gangs to terrorize innocent citizens. It's past time that people like Victor Borodini were exposed for the scum they really are, gangsters who've seized control of the city's outlying areas against the people's will and are using the people they're claiming to protect as hostages to keep themselves from being driven out. I'm personally serving notice on Victor Borodini that I'm going to do everything in my power to shut down his criminal operations in this city. And if either he or his son dare to show their faces outside their criminal enclave on Long Island, which I very much doubt they'll have the guts to do, they'll be arrested for conspiracy to commit murder, trafficking in drugs and stolen goods, black marketeering, kidnapping and violation of the federal racketeering statutes. And on behalf of the federal government, I'm extending an offer of a reward, protection and full immunity from prosecution to anyone who's willing to come forward with information leading to the arrest of Victor Borodini and his son, Tommy Borodini, or information relating to any of their criminal operations in this city. And if the Borodinis want to send any more of their hired killers after me, you tell them that I'm waiting."

"There you have it," Linda Tellerman said, turning to the camera. "The gauntlet's been thrown down. The battle lines are drawn and—"

Victor Borodini thumbed the remote control and turned off the TV in disgust, then threw the remote control unit across the room. He reached for the phone.

"Get Tommy in here," he snapped.

A moment later, the phone on Tommy Borodini's nightstand rang. He ignored it, concentrating his attentions on the energetic fourteen-year-old girl in bed with him, but the ringing was insistent. He swore and picked it up.

"What the hell *is* it?"

"Sorry to disturb you, Mr. Borodini," said the voice on the other end, "but it's your father. He wants to see you right away."

Tommy B took a deep breath and let it out slowly. A summons from the old man was not to be ignored.

"All right, tell him I'll be right there."

He started to get out of bed and pull his pants on.

"You're not going *now*?" the girl said. "Christ, I was almost *there*!"

"Shut up."

"Tommy . . ." she whined plaintively, reaching for his belt.

He twisted away. "Shut up, I said! Stay here. I'll be back."

He finished getting dressed, checked his appearance in the mirror, and then hurried to his father's wing of the estate. Unless there was specific business to be taken care of, he rarely saw his father, even though they lived in the same house. It was a very large house, more like a fortress, really, and they occupied separate wings of the estate. Tommy B showed his father the proper filial devotion and respect, as was expected of him, but he labored under no illusions that his father liked him, much less loved him. Nor did he really love his father, for that matter. Victor Borodini was not the sort of man who inspired love, even in his sons. What he inspired was fear. He knew it, enjoyed it, and made the most of it. He could put more menace into a few soft syllables than a dozen screamers in full howl could generate. And, as the eldest son, Tommy was somehow expected to live up to that. He did his best, but despite all his inherent viciousness, it was never quite enough.

His younger brothers, Rick and Paulie, had a much easier time of it, not being first in line for the throne. Rick, at twenty-six, had something of their father's class and style, for which Tommy hated him, because no matter how well he tried to dress, he still looked like a cheap hood while Rick looked like he stepped out of the pages of a fashion maga-zine. But Rick was empty. If there was anything going on upstairs, it was concealed behind a maze of walls. He seemed completely unemotional. And though he was not well liked, he could command respect. On numerous occasions, espe-cially in dealing with the street gangs, he had proved himself a good soldier in the Borodini family.

As for nineteen-year-old Paulie, he was much more like their departed mother, who had died of cancer when Paulie was just eight years old. He had her smouldering, dark good looks, but he was a fragile boy, quiet, passive, and submis-sive. Paulie was the kind of guy who, when he walked into a room, you got the feeling somebody just left. He was good at taking care of business, so long as it was done on paper. He was smart and detail oriented, but he simply couldn't handle people. He was walking wallpaper.

Tommy had once overheard a couple of the men talking, not knowing that he was within earshot, and one of them had laughingly suggested that Tommy, Rick and Paulie were like three separate fragments of one personality. Rick all cool and lethal competence, but cold and insubstantial as a shadow; Paulie smart as a whip, yet painfully shy, a nice guy, but basically a nebbish and a bit too feminine to suit their tastes; and Tommy, a seething cauldron of emotions, a firecracker with too short a fuse just waiting to blow up in someone's face. An icepick, a calculator and a hand grenade, the man had said. If the old man could've put 'em all together in one body, he might've really had something.

Tommy had not let on that he had overheard their conversation. Their comments rankled. He did not like to think of himself as lacking something that his brothers had. And it galled him that his father's people talked like that behind his back. Paulie would've probably agreed with them, the way he always tried to agree with everybody to avoid any kind of conflict. Rick probably wouldn't give a shit. But what they said had burned in Tommy's gut like a bleeding ulcer, and he became more determined than ever to prove them wrong.

He threw his weight around and handled his authority like a bludgeon, but all he succeeded in doing was reinforcing their opinion of him. He had their unquestioning obedience, but instead of treating him with respect, they tended to tiptoe around him like one would around a vicious dog that was liable to snap without warning and rip off a chunk of thigh. And though he didn't know it, they had bestowed another nickname on him. Tommy the Bug. As in bughouse. But they were very careful not to use it in his presence.

They still talked about the working over that he gave his girlfriend before he gave her to that pimp. Christ, he damn near killed her, then turned her over to some of his sleazy hairball grunts, sat there and watched them do her. Jesus. He was a fucking bug, all right. The old man would've burst a blood vessel if he'd known about that. All right, so the girl got out of line and cut him. But she was Family and you just don't treat Family that way. Hell, they'd been practically engaged, and Tommy'd thrown that other little chippie in her face. What the hell did he expect? A girl with any self-respect, what *else* could she have done? He had it coming. He was a bug and he had short eyes, besides. He'd never have the stuff to fill the old man's shoes.

Tommy knew they felt that way, though he didn't know the full extent of the distaste they felt for him. His father knew it, though. Victor Borodini turned a blind eye to much of what Tommy did, and he asked few questions because he didn't really want to hear the answers. He was fond of Paulie, because he reminded him of his late wife, and he felt Rick had potential, but Tommy was the one who'd have to take over when he was too old to run things. And maybe he could do it, too, if he could learn to control his goddamn temper and stop acting like a loose cannon. The way to help him do that, Borodini thought, was to give the boy responsibility. And though Tommy was a little crazy and a bit too heavy-handed, he had never let him down.

Till now.

"You wanted to see me, Papa?"

Victor Borodini did not reply at once. He simply sat there and gave his son a level stare, thinking, as if he could beam the message to him telepathically, "Come on, Tommy, look me in the eyes, God damn it." But no, Tommy met his stare for perhaps three seconds, and then, as always, he looked away.

"I gave you a job to do and you disappointed me," said Borodini quietly.

Tommy felt a knot forming in his stomach.

"I told you I wanted Steele taken care of," Borodini said. "So what did you do?"

Tommy swallowed nervously. "I sent Caravelli," he said. "You said you wanted to be sure. Caravelli's our best shooter—"

"One man," said Borodini dryly. "You sent one man against someone who took on a whole street gang like the Chingos by himself?" He snorted. "I just saw it on the news. That TV reporter, Linda Tellerman, was right there when it went down and she got it all on tape. Caravelli missed his shot and Steele nabbed him. And he got him to confess you were the one who sent him. You realize what that means?"

Tommy said nothing.

"It means that now there's a federal warrant out for your arrest," his father continued in a level tone. "And for *my* arrest as well. And it means they've got a witness who will testify against us. The warrant itself is of no concern to me. It's the mileage they can get from it that bothers me."

Tommy frowned. "I don't understand."

"No, I know you don't," said Borodini. "That's the trouble. There's a lot more to running this family than simply being strong, Tommy. You have to be smart as well. You have to know how to figure the odds and play the percentages. Right now, we're strong and the feds can't touch us, but that's not gonna last. We have to think about the future. Little by little, they're gonna start pulling this country back together. We've got a good thing going, but if we don't grow, sooner or later, they'll run right over us. Getting control of the gangs is only the first step. We need to control the city. We need to take over the power structure so that nobody, not the Delanos or the Pastoris or the Castellanos, or any of the other enclaves can get big enough to threaten us. And then if any of the other cities need to deal with Midtown, they'll have to deal with *us*.

"I need for you to understand this, Tommy," he continued. "The way to fight the establishment is to *become* the establishment. And you don't take over the establishment the way we took over the gangs. Force is only a small part of it. You've got to use the *people*. You've got to convince them that what you've got to offer is a better deal than what the competition's got. And once you've got the people on your side, you've got the competition licked—you see what I'm saying?"

"Yes, Papa."

"They can call us criminals," Borodini continued, "and they can accuse us of any damn thing they want, but the bottom line is if they haven't got the proof, if they haven't got something they can make stick in a court of law, they're just blowin' smoke. It won't stop them from coming after us, but it'll keep us looking good. They can say we run the gangs, and we can say we just do business with them. It's our right. And the harder the gangs get for the city to control, the more the people will start wondering if maybe we couldn't do a better job, because we *can* do business with them.

"They'll look at the crime rate they've got, and they'll think, the Borodini enclave *has* no crime. The Borodinis can give their people security. They'll look at the problems that they've got with shortages, and they'll think, the Borodini enclave *has* no shortages. They can do business with the Brood, they can do business with the freebooters, they can do business with anyone it takes to get their people taken care of. Why can't the city do that?

"And they'll start to think that maybe everything that I've been saying in the papers and on the talk shows is all true. Maybe the feds are really after me because I took control of this part of the Island when they turned their back on it and I'm doing a better job of taking care of things than they are. And maybe they're afraid of the people finding out that I could run their city better than they can, and they're trying to blame me for all their problems because they're afraid of the people finding out the truth. And maybe the people will start wondering if it's true what I've been saying, that the city administration is corrupt and putting off the blame on me. And maybe they'll start wondering if they shouldn't have a better choice. You understand what I'm saying, Tommy? We wouldn't have to take over the city by force. The people would invite us in.

"But that won't happen if the feds can hit us with charges they can make stick," he continued. "It won't happen if we start looking bad. It won't happen if someone like Steele captures their imaginations and becomes a hero to them. They'll start to listen when that fucking robot goes on TV and calls me a maggot and a slime. And they'll start to think that maybe Victor Borodini isn't the answer to their problems, but more cyborgs like Steele are. You understand what I'm saying, Tommy? If the people accept that idea, we'll have a pile of trouble on our hands, and everything I've worked for all these years will turn to shit. And I'm not about to let that happen. I want Steele taken out for keeps. I want him put down so hard there's nothing left of him for them to rebuild—you understand me?''

"What about Caravelli?" Tommy asked.

"Don't you concern yourself with him," said the elder Borodini. "I'll put out the word and make sure that squealer's made an example of. You just worry about Steele."

"I'll take care of it, Papa," Tommy said. "I'll go make sure there won't be no mistakes this time."

"There'd better not be," Borodini said. "One is all you get."

7

Phillip Gates arrived at Dev's apartment promptly at eight. He took one look at Dev and frowned. "God, Dev, you look awful. What's wrong?"

"I haven't slept, that's all," said Dev. "That and the anxiety."

"Over what? What's so bad that you couldn't tell me over the phone?"

"I want you to listen to something," Dev said, conducting Gates into the den, where his computer was set up.

"What is it? Is it the program?"

"Yeah. Sit down. You want a drink?"

"Sure, why not?"

Dev got out the bottle of Scotch he'd gone out and bought twenty minutes earlier.

"I've been working with the program," he said, "conducting therapy sessions with it much as I've done with Steele. Only this time, I've done something different. For a while now, I've had the nagging feeling that there was something bothering Steele, something he wasn't telling me. Steele doesn't like psychiatrists very much. The two of us get along okay and we've managed to establish a rapport of sorts, but he never has been completely comfortable with me. He keeps his guard up."

He handed Gates his drink.

"At first, I thought it was because he was a Strike Force cop," Dev continued. "They're evaluated constantly by psychiatrists in Internal Affairs. They see a lot of dangerous duty and they're often under great stress. And since an IAD doctor can have them removed from duty, either temporarily or permanently, they learn to be very cautious during their evaluations, and they spend so much time with shrinks that they get good at playing the game and keeping their defenses up. I thought Steele's antipathy towards psychiatrists was a result of that, but I didn't want to take anything for granted, so I've been doin' some careful checking into his background.''

"And what did you find out?'' asked Gates.

"Steele's mother was killed when he was just a boy,'' said Dev. "It must have been a tremendously traumatic experience for him. She was a hospital nurse, and she became infected with Virus 3 when she came in contact with a sample of contaminated blood. She became a screamer, and she came home to her family and attacked her children. Steele was spared, but she managed to get to his two younger brothers before his father could stop her. She apparently bit them repeatedly, and they were both infected with the virus. Steele's father struggled with her and was finally forced to shoot her, but not before he became infected himself. So to spare his sons the agonies of becoming screamers, he shot them both and then turned the gun on himself. Steele witnessed the whole thing.''

"Jesus,'' Gates said.

"Steele became a ward of the state,'' said Dev. "And after what happened, he spent some time in a hospital psychiatric ward. It seems the doctor who worked with him was somewhat heavy-handed. Steele had blocked out what had happened to his family, and his therapist worked pretty hard to make him confront it. Apparently, too hard. He was successful, but Steele's had a dislike of psychiatrists ever since. And though we've made some good progress, when it comes to certain things, he just won't open up. And if I tried to force the issue, it would only make things worse.''

"I see your point,'' said Gates. "So what's all this leading up to?''

"After I started workin' with the backup program you gave me,'' Dev said, "I began encountering the same problem. So I had a long talk with Dr. Nakamura. She showed me how to write in an imperative that would circumvent Steele's reluctance to open up. Sort of like a computer version of hypnosis, in a way, that would force the program to respond. Steele would never have agreed to anything like that, of course, and I had some misgivings about whether or not I should do it with the program. I'm not at all certain about the ethics of this situation. But I figured in the end that if it would help Steele, then it was worth a try. So I went ahead and did it.''

He went over to the computer and booted up the program.

"I want you to listen to this and tell me what you think,'' he said. "Don't say anything. Just listen.'' He switched on the voice synthesizer and the microphone. "Steele? Can you hear me?''

Steele's voice came from the speaker. "Yes, I can hear you.''

Dev switched off the mike for a moment. "He thinks he's under mild sedation,'' he explained. "It's what I told him to explain why he can't see or feel anything. He doesn't realize that he's only a backup program. I decided not to tell him that because I didn't want to agitate him.''

Gates frowned. Cooper was talking about the program as if it were alive and self-aware. But it was only a computer program. Data. Mental engrams. He didn't think it was possible for it to become "agitated.''

Dev switched on the mike again. "I'd like to talk about your dream again,'' he said. "You know, the recurring one you told me about before.''

There was a slight pause. "Okay.''

"I'd like to go over it one more time, from the beginning,'' Dev said. "Tell me about it.''

Another slight pause, a bit longer this time. "Well . . . I'm in the park.''

"Central Park?''

"I . . . I don't know. It's just a park, I guess. It could be Central Park, I suppose, but I'm not really sure.''

"Okay. Go on.''

Gates put down his drink and leaned forward with interest. The program was not responding at all the way he had expected it to. In his work with it, he had never actually spoken with it the way Dev was doing now. He had worked with it on a display screen, pulling out certain sections of data and examining it, programming it into Steele's cybernetic brain as separate files designed to interface with one another. He had never actually communicated with the program directly or tried to examine the subconscious engrams in detail. There had been no reason to do so, and it simply never occurred to him.

"Well, I'm in the park," the program continued, responding in Steele's voice, "and my family is with me. The kids are playing with the dog. And my wife is sitting on the blanket, setting out our picnic lunch. Only there's something wrong."

Another pause.

"Go on," prompted Dev. "What's wrong?"

The program hesitated once more. "We never had a dog," the program said. "And we have only two kids. Jason and Cory. But in the dream, I've got three kids, two boys and a girl. And the boys are twins. They're calling me Daddy, but I don't know any of their names."

"You don't know or you can't remember?" Dev asked.

"I . . . don't know. I mean, I don't know which it is. I suppose I can't remember, because at first I couldn't remember my wife's name, either, only now I can. It's Donna."

"But I thought your wife's name was Janice," Dev said.

"It was. I mean, it is. And that's another thing. Janice was a blonde. This woman's a brunette. And she doesn't look anything like Janice. Her name is Donna, but that's all I know about her. I don't know who she is."

"But you referred to her as your wife," said Dev.

"I know. That's the part that makes no sense. I'm there with her, and with the kids, and I feel that she's my wife and they're my kids . . . but I don't *know* them!"

"Okay, go on. What happens next?"

"The kids are playing. Tossing a frisbee with the dog. The dog is jumping up and catching it in its mouth. I don't know the dog's name, either, but it seems like it's my dog. It's very confusing. Then, suddenly, my mother's there."

"You know her?" said Dev.

"Yeah, it's my real mother. She just appears suddenly out of nowhere. And it's dark. Late evening, I'd say. A second ago, it was daylight. Now it's dark. It just changed, all of a sudden."

"But you're still in the park?"

"Yeah, I'm still in the park."

"What does your mother look like?"

"The same way she looked when . . . when I was just a kid. The last time I ever saw her. She . . . she's a screamer. She's got running sores all over her face. Her clothes are all torn up and filthy, like she's been clawing at them. She looks terrible. She starts attacking the kids. It's horrible."

"Your two brothers?" Dev asked.

"No, no, the twins. And the little girl. They're screaming. She's biting them. My wife is screaming my name. . . ."

"What name?" said Dev, suddenly alert.

"My name. . . ."

"What name is she screaming? Can you hear the name? Tell me the *name*."

Gates was gripping the arms of his chair tightly.

"I . . . I don't. . . ."

"What name is she screaming? Listen to her! Tell me what you hear!"

"Jon . . . Jonathan. She's screaming 'Jonathan.' "

"Is that you?" asked Dev. "Are you Jonathan?"

"I . . . I can't . . . I don't want to talk about this anymore."

"We're almost finished," Dev said. "Just tell me, are you Jonathan?"

"No. I . . . I don't know who Jonathan is. But she's screaming at me and I can't move and she . . . she . . . that's it. There isn't any more."

"But there *is* more, isn't there?" asked Dev.

"I'm tired. I want to go to sleep."

"Just tell me the rest of the dream."

"I can't. I . . . I don't remember. That's all there is. Can't I go back to sleep now?"

"Okay," said Dev. "That's all for now. Go back to sleep."

He turned off the mike and quit the program. Gates was looking at him intently.

"I don't know what the hell to make of that," he said. "You said this has happened before?"

"We've been over the dream several times now," Dev said, "but just now was the first time we got the name Jonathan. That's something new. We're making progress."

Gates looked worried. "Hell, I wouldn't call that progress," he said. "It doesn't make any sense. There must be some sort of glitch in the program."

"I don't think so," Dev said. "At least, not a glitch in the way you'd think of it. Something's definitely wrong, that much is true, but it's not a glitch. You put it there."

"*I* put it there?" said Gates.

"That's right," said Dev. "When you downloaded the data from Steele's organic brain, you compensated for the damage resulting from his injuries with data you'd downloaded from other individuals in previous experiments. You incorporated that data into Steele's mental engrams. What I believe is happening is that that data is now expressing itself through his subconscious. Steele's mental engrams have essentially been contaminated in the programming by the mental engrams of other individuals, and he is now manifesting traces of their memories. At least one of them, anyway. His brain is being haunted by cybernetic ghosts."

"That's impossible," said Gates.

"You just heard it," Dev said.

"There's got to be some other explanation," Gates said, shaking his head. "The auxiliary data was carefully incorporated into the engram matrix. It was designed to facilitate his emotional responsivity. He can't be experiencing direct sensory impressions downloaded from other test subjects. We used only bits and pieces of various other engram files—"

"Apparently, that was enough," said Dev. "You simply can't break down the subconscious the way you can computer data, Phil. It's too complex. Too . . . ethereal. You told me yourself that this was an exact duplicate of the data Steele was programmed with. That means that if it's in there, it's in Steele's cybernetic brain. This is what he's been keeping from me. He's been having that dream. He's experiencing the memories of at least one of the test subjects whose mental engrams were used to complete his matrix. Possibly, what he's experiencing is some sort of a composite memory fragment, I really have no way of knowing. And I have no way of knowing if this process will continue. It's possible that his personality may be fragmenting.''

"Does Higgins know about this?" asked Gates.

Dev shook his head. "I haven't told him yet. Frankly, I'm not sure if I should. Technically, I suppose I'm breaching the confidentiality of the doctor/patient relationship by telling you, but I need some help with this, and I didn't know what else to do.''

"Dev, that's just a program," Gates said. "You're not breaking confidentiality. It's not a patient, for God's sake, it's only data.''

"*Is* it?" Dev asked. "That data, as you call it, happens to be Steele's personality. The sum total of who and what he is. It's his *identity*. An exact duplicate, an electronic clone. And it's *alive*. Perhaps not in the same sense as you and I are alive, but it's alive just the same. You heard it. It's self-aware. It's Steele's exact twin, it merely lacks a body. You've been working with Artificial Intelligence programs for so long, Phil, that you tend to think of Steele's mental engrams as nothing but a very sophisticated AI program, but it's not. It isn't artificial intelligence, it's *real* intelligence, a human personality translated to software. While I was talking to it, asking it questions, it *hesitated*. Computer programs don't hesitate. It was functioning under a programmed imperative, and it was *still* hesitating. It was fighting me, especially right near the end. Does a computer program say, 'I don't want to talk about it,' when you ask it a question? Even the most sophisticated AI program?''

"No," said Gates softly. "It doesn't. It can't.''

"Only this one can," said Dev. "I don't think you fully realized the implications of what you did when you made this backup copy for me. What happens when it finds out that it's not Steele, but merely an electronic clone stored in a computer? What do I tell it? What do I *do*, Phil? And what happens if we erase it? Won't that be murder?''

"You're overreacting," Gates said. "How can it be murder? It's not really alive in any traditional sense. Was it birth when we made the copy?''

"I don't know," said Dev. "Maybe it was."

"Nonsense. You've been pushing yourself too hard, Dev. You're getting carried away with this whole thing. You've got to step back from it and relax. Try to get some rest."

"How can I?" Dev said, sitting down with a heavy sigh and picking up his drink. "I'm breakin' entirely new ground here, Phil. And I haven't got a thing to guide me. We've taken a man's personality, his very soul, and we've made a copy of it. Think what that means."

"Dev, it's only data—"

"It *isn't* only data! Is that all a human personality is to you, just *data*? That's Steele in there! And Steele's a human being, he isn't a machine!"

"Isn't he?" said Gates. "Look, Dev, between you, me and the walls here, the bottom line is that Steele died. He *died*, you understand what I'm saying? He was a vegetable and he died the minute we removed his brain. Brain death is legally considered death, Dev. You can keep the body alive with life support machines, but once the brain is gone, that's it. Nobody's home. It's finished. We took Steele's body, augmented it with mechanical parts, implanted a cybernetic brain and programmed it with data we downloaded from his mind, but it's only *data*, Dev. Steele is a machine. A machine that's partly flesh and blood, that's true. His body still has organic functions, but it's essentially no different from when it was on life support systems while he was in a coma. He isn't human, Dev. He's a cyborg running on a cybernetic brain programmed with the most sophisticated software yet devised, but it's still software. That's all it is."

Dev stared at him for a long moment.

"You really believe that, don't you?"

"It's the truth, Dev."

"Have you tried telling that to Steele?"

"No, of course not," Gates said. "It's important to the project that for Steele to function at optimal levels, he needs to believe he's human. And it's important for him to be perceived that way in terms of public relations as well. It wouldn't go over very well if the public perceived what we're doing as turning dead people into robots. So, for the record, Steele is 'human,' okay? But that doesn't change the facts. A program is a program. Software is still nothing more than software. It isn't self-aware, and it certainly isn't alive. It's merely got some sort of glitch in it, that's all. We'll pull him in and fix it.''

"No," said Dev.

"What do you mean, no? You just said yourself that you're afraid Steele's personality might be fragmenting. We need to find the glitch and correct it before the problem can get any worse."

"I don't think you *can* correct it," Dev said.

"Look, Dev, with all due respect, you're not a cybernetics engineer—"

"And you're not a psychiatrist," said Dev. "You're lookin' at this thing with an engineer's mentality, Phil, seein' things in simple, logical terms of black and white. But the subconscious isn't logical. We're dealin' with a lot of gray areas. How can you be sure that if you tinker with the program and eliminate this 'glitch,' as you put it, you won't also eliminate some very fundamental part of Steele's personality?''

"So what if we do?" said Gates. "We'll compensate for it. So long as his ability to function remains unimpaired—"

"Damn it, Phil, you just don't understand! Steele *isn't* a machine! You don't even realize the significance of what you've achieved! You didn't simply write some kind of complicated computer program, you downloaded *human* mental engrams and loaded them into an artificial brain! You've effected an intelligence transplant! No artificial intelligence, but *human* intelligence! You sat here and you listened to me interact with that program. You heard how the program responded. How can you deny that it's alive and self-aware? How can you fail to accept it?

"Or maybe you just don't *want* to accept it," Dev continued, suddenly struck by the insight. "Maybe seein' Steele as a machine is what keeps you from havin' to grapple with the philosophical implications of what you've done. That makes it simple for you, doesn't it? The whole thing is reduced to an engineering problem. Mechanical and mathematical problems and solutions. The human element simply doesn't enter into it. Only Susan Carmody didn't feel that way about him, did she? She fell in love with him. Are you tellin' me that she fell in love with a machine?''

Gates did not respond for a long moment. Finally, he said, ''Dr. Carmody was under a great deal of pressure.''

''So what are you sayin', she relieved her tensions with the most sophisticated sex toy ever made?'' said Dev. ''Or that she committed high-tech necrophilia?''

''You don't have to be crude,'' said Gates with a grimace.

''I'll be anything I have to be in order to get through to you,'' said Dev. He pointed to the computer. ''That program is alive. And Steele is in trouble. And it's trouble you can't solve with an engineering fix. You didn't write that program, Gates. Nature did. You just moved it from one place to another. And you managed to disrupt it in the process. Now *I'm* the one who's goin' to have to fix it, and I don't know how I'm goin' to do it. I'm trained to deal with schizophrenia, with neurosis, with delusional systems of belief, only what Steele is experiencing is not delusional, it's *real*. That woman named Donna and those three children and that dog are not figments of his imagination, they're real, or they *were* real to someone, perhaps to several people, and now they're real to him as well because they're part of him. Donna *is* his wife, because she was married to someone whose downloaded mental engrams were used to supplement Steele's matrix. He knows her, yet he doesn't know her. She's a part of him, and yet he's never even met her. He's experiencing someone else's memory, only it's now become his memory as well, his experience, only it never happened to him. And if I can't find a way to help him resolve that in his mind, it's goin' to drive him crazy.''

Gates stared at the melting ice in his glass. He didn't know what to think. His mind was in a turmoil.

''I . . . I'm not sure about any of this,'' he said. ''I don't know what's happening, but whatever it is, Higgins will have to be told about this immediately.''

''No, absolutely not,'' said Dev. ''I can't allow it.''

"What do you mean, you can't *allow* it?" Gates said. "It isn't your decision. Higgins *has* to know."

"We can't pass the buck on this one, Phil," said Dev. "Unloading it on Higgins won't do either of us any good, and it certainly won't do Steele any good. What can Higgins do? He'll hit the ball right back into your court. He'll pull Steele in and order us to work together to debug his program. Only that's not the way to solve this problem. We can't simply erase it. Maybe you can, but I can't sit still for it. Steele is still my patient and I have a responsibility to him."

"You're not the only one who's got responsibilities, you know," said Gates. "I've got to answer to Higgins. I can't keep something like this from him. I'm sorry, Dev, I simply can't. I've got to tell him."

"Then I'll have you brought up on charges for violating security by givin' me an unauthorized copy of top secret government data," Dev said.

Gates snorted. "Don't be a fool. You're just as guilty of violating security as I am. You'd be throwing yourself right in the fire with me."

"I don't care. I'm willin' to take my chances. Are you?"

Gates stared at him. "You'd really do that?"

"Try me."

"You son of a bitch. And I thought you were my friend."

"I *am* your friend, Phil. And I'm sorry. I truly am. But you're puttin' me in a position where I have no other choice. Ethically, I'm bound to protect my patient. And if you force my hand, I'm willin' to go to the wall on this one."

Gates sighed with resignation. "All right. What do you want from me?"

"I need your help, Phil. As you said, I'm not a cybernetics engineer. And you're not a psychiatrist. But between the two of us, maybe we can find a way to stop what's happening to Steele." Dev turned to the computer. "And maybe he can help us do it."

"*He*?" said Gates.

"That's right, Phil. He," Dev said, staring at the backup copy of the program still loaded into the computer. "God help him."

• • •

It was getting late and Ice had left to go to his own apartment downstairs. They had been listening to Raven for hours, with Steele asking countless questions, trying to find out everything she knew about the Borodinis.

"You gotta promise me one thing," said Raven, sitting at the table across from Steele, a drink in front of her. "When you go up against the Borodinis, I want to be there."

"Forget it," Steele said.

"But I can help you!"

"You can also get yourself killed," said Steele.

"I can take care of myself."

"Look, after what Tommy B did to you, I can appreciate how you feel," said Steele, "but I'm going to have my hands full as it is. You'll slow us down, and I can't be worrying about you."

"I didn't ask you to worry about me," she said. "Why should you care, anyway? Just give me a gun, and I'll look out for myself."

"You want to commit suicide, that's your business," Steele said, "but I'm not about to help you do it."

"Damn it, Steele, I—"

The phone rang. Steele went to pick it up. "I don't want to discuss it," he said. "Hello?"

"Steele? Ron Jaworski, over at the Project. Dr. Gates had me assemble a file for you on the Borodini family."

"Right. You got it for me?"

"I've got it. I can let you have a high-speed download. You ready?"

"Go ahead."

"Hold on a sec. Okay, here comes. . . ."

The data hummed through the receiver with a soft, barely audible whine as Steele listened, his cybernetic brain taking the download and recording it. Seconds later, a high-pitched tone indicated that the run was complete.

The tech came back on the line. "You got it?"

"I've got it. Thanks."

"Will you be needing anything else or can I clock out now?"

"No, that'll be all for tonight. Go on home, Jaworski. And thanks again."

"No problem. Anytime."

Steele hung up the phone. He now knew everything that was officially known about the Borodinis and their enclave. But Raven had told him some things that weren't in any file. He turned around.

"There's still some things I haven't told you," she said. "Things you'll need to know. But I won't tell you any more unless you promise that you'll take me with you."

"Fine," said Steele. "Have it your way. You can pack your things. I'll call security and have them let you out. Thanks for the help."

She stared at him. "You bastard. You're not kickin' me outta here! You told me I could help!"

"It's up to you," said Steele. "You cooperate, you can stay. You start giving me ultimatums, the door's right over there."

Her expression softened, and she came over to him. "I don't want to leave," she said. "I want to help you. I just want to see Tommy B get what's comin' to him."

She took his hand and lifted it up to her lips.

"I can help you, Steele," she said. "We could be good together."

She gazed into his eyes and slipped his index finger into her mouth. She tongued it gently as her fingertips caressed his palm. Then her expression changed.

"What's this?"

Her stroking fingertips had found the gunport in his palm. She looked at it, puzzled, then glanced up at him.

"What *is* that?"

By way of reply, Steele slid the gun barrel out through his palm. She jerked back, dropping his hand.

"What the hell . . . ?"

She stared at him, then at his hand. He held it out so she could see.

"Is that a *gun*?" she asked.

Steele nodded.

"You've got a *gun* built into your arm?"

He switched on his laser designator and his eyes glowed with two bright pinpoints of light.

Raven slowly backed away from him. "Jesus fuckin' Christ . . . what the hell *are* you?"

"Still think we could be good together, Raven?"

He retracted the gun barrel, then released the lock on his right hand. As it dropped off, he caught it with his left hand and tossed it to her.

"You want a pacifier? Here, take it with you."

She instinctively caught the hand, then cried out and dropped it to the floor. She stared at it, wide-eyed, lying at her feet, then looked up at Steele, her jaw slack.

"You're a fuckin' robot?" she said with disbelief.

"I'm a cyborg," Steele said. "Don't you watch the news or read the papers?"

She shook her head, stunned. "What . . . what the hell's a cyborg? You some kind of a *machine*?"

"Part machine, part human," Steele said.

She raised her arm hesitantly and pointed at his eyes. "Turn that off, willya? It's weird."

The lights in Steele's eyes winked out.

She stared at him, shaking her head slowly. "Jesus. Jesus God . . ."

She knelt down and carefully picked up his hand, examining it.

"It . . . it feels so *real!*"

"Nysteel and polymer," he said, "with sophisticated nerve sensors built in."

"I can't believe it," she said softly, awestruck. She glanced up at him with astonishment. "You mean somebody *built* you?"

"Not exactly," Steele said. "I was a cop. Borodini's people ambushed me and left me for dead, but they didn't quite finish the job. I was brain damaged, in a coma. The feds took me and fixed me up, using some artificial parts. Then they took all the information from my brain and loaded it into a computer. And then they stuck it in my skull. My skeletal structure was reinforced with nysteel alloy, my arms and legs are state-of-the-art, fusion-powered nysteel prosthetics with built-in weapons systems, and my polymer skin makes me almost completely bulletproof. My skull casing is nysteel and can take a hit that would kill an ordinary man. But you're *not* bulletproof, are you? You see why I don't want you involved?''

She came up to him hesitantly and gave him back his hand. She couldn't take her eyes off the gleaming nysteel armature exposed at his wrist and the 10 mm. gunbarrel that protruded from it slightly. Steele snapped his hand back on and it locked into place. She gazed up into his eyes.

"Are they . . . ?"

"Artificial," Steele said. "Bionic optics units. What you just saw was the built-in laser designator system that lets me lock on target. I can't miss. I'm like a walking tank, Raven. I'm very hard to kill. Can you say the same for yourself?"

She reached up carefully and touched his face. "Is that . . . fake?"

"No, that's real," Steele said.

Her hand went down to his open shirt and touched his chest. "And that?"

"That's polymer," he said. "it's a sort of plastic skin graft. The ribs underneath are nysteel alloy, but the organs and the muscles are all real."

She gently stroked his chest with her fingernails. "Can you feel that?"

"Yes, I can feel it. I feel things the same way you do. And I think the same way you do, too, only I can do it much faster."

Her hand started to drop lower. He stopped her before it passed his waist.

She glanced up at him, questioningly.

"Yeah. That's real, too," he said wryly.

"Wow," she said. "You mean you're like a real person, only with artificial arms and legs and stuff? Like . . . like somebody who's handicapped?"

"I suppose you could look at it that way," said Steele. "Only I've got an artificial brain as well."

"Jesus, this is blowin' my mind," she said, staring at him with fascination. "How could they *do* that?"

"You know what an interface is?" asked Steele.

She shook her head.

"It's like when they connect up two computers so they can talk to each other," Steele explained.

"Oh, yeah. Okay."

"Well, they've been working on a way to interface a human brain and a computer," Steele said, "so that a computer can talk to a brain and vice versa. To help people learn things faster. They do it by putting a little computer chip into your head. That's what they did with me. I was working with them on an experiment in brain/computer interface. They wanted to see if the things I learned during my years as a Strike Force cop could be taken from my mind and put on a computer, so that other people could learn the same things, only much faster."

"Wow. And does it work?"

"Yeah, it works. When Borodini's people shot me up, I was taken to the project lab, and they used that little chip inside my head to take everything out of my mind and store it in a computer. Then they put an experimental computer brain into my head and programmed it with my own personality. My own memories. Everything my human brain contained. So I still feel the same way I always did, I still think the same way, I still have the same memories and personality, but it's all stored inside a cybernetic brain."

"Jesus, what a trip," she said. "What's it like?"

"It doesn't frighten you?" asked Steele.

"Hey, when it comes to some of the shit I've seen, you don't even *qualify* as scary. Besides, I've done tricks with people who were handicapped. What's the big deal? They're people, same as anybody else. They just got some parts missin'."

"Like a brain?" said Steele.

"Yeah, well, okay, I gotta admit that's a new one on me. But I wouldn't exactly call that scary. It's pretty fuckin' weird, but it doesn't scare me. Why should it? You've treated me lots better than most guys I've been with."

There it was, thought Steele. Simple as that. Acceptance. He marveled at it. Janice, a woman he'd lived with for almost twenty years, hadn't even tried. She'd divorced him and left the city rather than face the prospect of being married to some sort of freak and having her kids, in her own words, have "some kind of robot for a father." Shelley Taylor, his best friend's sister, whom he'd known for more than twenty years, had not even been able to look him in the eyes and had been profoundly uncomfortable in his presence. Her relief when he had left had been all too painfully visible.

And now this girl, whom he scarcely knew at all, had seemingly accepted him for what he was in a mere matter of moments. But perhaps it was because, as she herself had said, that after some of the things she'd seen and been through, he didn't even qualify as scary. On that level, though they came from different worlds, they could understand each other. Both of them were damaged goods.

Her initial response to him had been predictable, dictated by the law of the urban jungle. In her world, women were nothing more than chattel. She understood being whacked around and degraded and, in her twisted worldview, anyone not man enough to do that was going to get victimized himself. And he deserved whatever was coming to him. It was a dog-eat-dog world, eat or be eaten, beat or be beaten. And when Steele had not followed the laws of the equation, she had tried to rip him off. Had even tried to kill him. But, in his own way, he had asserted the law of the jungle over her. Not by slapping her around as if she were a piece of meat, to which she would have responded like the animal she was, submissive in the face of violent domination, yet ready to tear his throat out the moment that his back was turned, but by a simple and direct, non-violent assertion of his superior strength and confidence. Like a larger animal responding to a smaller, aggressive one encountered on its turf, drawing itself up and revealing its superior power without resorting to its use. Laying down the law. This is my territory. You don't bother me and I won't bother you. But challenge me, and I'll crush you into the ground.

And so they had achieved a sort of coexistence. Sharing the same space without threatening each other. It was not exactly a relationship, but for animals, just as for some people, it was a way to live. Only Steele felt there had to be more to life than that.

Tommy Borodini had a lot to answer for.

"You asked me what it's like," he said to her. "You really want to know?"

"Yeah. Sure, why not?"

"What's it like to be a hooker?" he asked.

She rolled her eyes. "Oh, Christ, you're not gonna be one of *those*, are you?"

He shook his head. "You don't understand," he said. "I'm not asking you how a nice girl like you got into a business like this. Besides, I already know how you got into it. I'm trying to make a point."

"Yeah, what's that?"

"When you turn a trick with someone, what's that like? Do you feel anything for him, except, perhaps, contempt? Does he feel anything for you except a temporary lust? He uses you and you use him. And when it's over, neither one of you wants anything to do with one another. In some ways, it's a lot like that."

She frowned. "I don't get you. How is it the same?"

"People treat you the same way," Steele said. "Like you're a machine. They care only about the uses they can put you to."

He got up and wandered out onto the balcony. She followed him.

"There was one exception," he said. He looked down at the floor. "She died right here."

"What happened?" Raven asked from behind him.

Steele looked out over the night lights of the city.

"It was Borodini," he said. "He tried to have me hit from a chopper." He glanced up toward the roof. "That's why there are gun turrets up there now. They didn't manage to kill me, but they got Susan. The only person who didn't treat me as if I were some kind of robot."

"What about Ice?" asked Raven.

Steele smiled. "Ice is a whole 'nother smoke, as my Texan shrink would say," he said. "He respects me precisely because I am what I am. He's something of a machine himself,

in some ways. I actually think he'd *like* being me. Yet I'd
trade places with him in a second.''

"That night you had the dream," said Raven. "Was it
about her? About what happened?''

Steele glanced away. "No. It was something else.''

He debated for a moment whether or not he should confide
in her. He felt a strong need to tell someone. And there was
no one else he could tell. No one except for Father Liam
Casey, whom he had already overburdened with his troubles
and from whom he was determined to stay away until this
thing with Borodini was resolved. He didn't want anyone else
to die on his account.

"You don't have to tell me if you don't want to,'' she said.

He looked at her. "No, it's okay. I want to.''

The night seemed to drag on endlessly as he walked the
fence along the north edge of the field, his assault rifle
cradled in the crook of his elbow. The crescent moon glowed
dimly in the night sky, and a cool breeze rustled through the
stalks behind him. He was bored out of his mind.

He'd joined the army expecting something a bit more
glamorous than this. The enlistment officer had promised
him, had *guaranteed* him, assignment to the Armored Corps,
and he'd pictured himself in a well-worn leather bomber's
jacket with a white silk scarf around his neck, riding convoy
escort duty along the long stretches of deserted highway
linking the cities with the outland settlements, guarding the
precious supply runs that kept the cities fed, living the adven-
turous life of an armor jockey, respected and admired by the
burly truck drivers and the slender, lissome exotic dancers
who entertained them at the fortified depots on the highways.

Instead, he'd been assigned to an infantry unit posted to an
agro-commune in upstate New York, and here he was, walking his rounds in the middle of the night, guarding a fucking
corn field. In another couple of hours, it would be oh-six-
hundred and his relief would arrive and he'd trudge back to
the Quonset hut barracks for a few drinks of whiskey with the
other soldiers getting off their shift and then some sack time.
Real glamorous. Join the army and be a fucking night watch-

man. Protect the corn from crows and field mice. Jesus, what a joke.

Ostensibly, he was supposed to be guarding the fields from roving bands of raiders, outlaw bands who roamed the countryside, attacking farms and outlying settlements, but no band of derelicts would dare attack a farm protected by an army unit, and there'd been no reports of screamers in the area for months. There was nothing to do but pull your duty, play cards, drink, shoot the bull, and sleep.

Every now and then, you'd get a weekend pass to go into town and spend an hour or two with one of the local hookers who charged a lot more than they were worth because it was a seller's market. There weren't any women in his unit, and the local girls, for the most part, steered clear of soldiers because being seen with one was a good way to get a "reputation." The only guys who had any real chance of getting one were the officers, and even they had precious little chance of getting in their pants unless they came up with a ring. There were a few good-looking girls who worked the farm, but orders prohibited fraternization with the females in the work crews on the principle that it could cause trouble among the men and with the girls' families, so all you could do was stand and drool over some tight-assed country girl in a halter top and skin-tight cutoffs while she fed the chickens or worked the fields you so valiantly protected. It was enough to make a guy crazy.

He glanced at his watch. God, the night was dragging! He reached into his shirt pocket and pulled out a pack of cigarettes. He lit one and inhaled deeply. You weren't supposed to smoke on guard duty, but fuck it. Half the time, the guys would sneak down among the rows of corn and kip out for a while. But if you did that, there was a chance of getting caught, though the officer of the guard hardly ever came out to check the fields. Still, just to be on the safe side, he cupped his hand around the cigarette to hide its telltale glow, just in case.

"Hi."

He spun around, startled, bringing up his gun.

A young blonde in tight jeans and a faded denim jacket was

leaning on the fence behind him. He recognized her as one of the girls who worked the farm. The foreman's daughter. She wore a tight tee-shirt beneath the open jacket. Her nipples were clearly outlined. God, she had great tits! He hadn't even heard her come up.

"Jesus, you gave me a start! What are you doing out here this time of night?"

She shrugged. "Couldn't sleep. Thought I'd take a walk. You got a spare smoke?"

He shook a cigarette out of the pack and offered it to her. She took it and he lit it for her.

"My name's Claire."

"I know. I've seen you around."

She smiled knowingly. "Yeah. I've seen you watching me."

He grinned. "It's hard not to."

She looked straight at him. "So. You like what you see?"

"Yes. Very much."

"I knew you'd be on guard duty tonight," she said. "It's a warm night, isn't it?"

She slowly removed her denim jacket, stretching so that her lush young breasts strained the fabric of the tee-shirt. The effect was not lost on him. She draped the jacket over the fence.

"My dad would kill me if he knew that I was out here talking to you," she said.

"What he doesn't know won't hurt him."

"You think I've got a nice body?"

"I think you've got a terrific body."

"Then why don't you put down that gun and come on over here?"

He didn't need a second invitation. He leaned the assault rifle up against the fence and went up to her. He took her in his arms. Her lips felt warm and moist, and he felt the heat surge through him as she slipped her tongue into his mouth. He ran his hands up underneath her tee-shirt, feeling her firm young breasts, and she moaned softly as she dropped her hands down to his belt and started to undo it. He couldn't believe this was happening. He devoured her mouth as she unbuttoned his fly and slipped her hand down inside his shorts. He groaned as he felt her fingers close around his shaft and start stroking rhythmically. His fingers fumbled with the buttons on her jeans. Then she pulled away from him, and with a knowing smile, slowly went down to her knees. He closed his eyes and moaned as she took him in her mouth. For a brief instant, paranoia surged through him as he thought about what would happen if they were caught together, an underage young girl, the foreman's daughter, no less, and then he didn't care as he felt her warm mouth enveloping him. As she sucked him, she pulled his pants down around his ankles and then urged him down onto the ground. She kneeled over him, pulled off her tee-shirt, then stood and quickly removed her jeans. She wasn't wearing anything underneath. She straddled him, slipped him inside her and started rocking back and forth, moving her pelvis against him, her face tilted backward, her eyes closed, her mouth open as she made soft, groaning sounds.

There was a brief, hissing noise and the arrow pierced her chest with a sound like a hammer striking meat. The razor-sharp, triangular head came ploughing through her back and burst through her chest, between her breasts. Warm blood spattered down into his face. Her eyes opened wide and she made a grunting sound, then fell forward onto his chest.

He cried out as the sharp arrowhead protruding from her chest broke his skin and struggled to push her off him, but she was dead weight and he was pinned. He heard the sounds of running footsteps coming up fast, and in a panic, he rolled, dislodging her body, and scrambled for his rifle. With his pants down around his ankles, he tripped and fell sprawling, then crawled forward quickly on his hands and knees, the adrenalin trip-hammering through him. A shot cracked out and he felt a bullet graze his shoulder. He cried out with pain, and his hand closed around the rifle stock. And then they were on him.

Steele sat up in bed with a start, crying out.

"It's okay, it's okay," Raven said, her hands on his shoulders. "It was just another nightmare, that's all. You're all right now."

Steele shut his eyes and exhaled heavily. She put her arms around him and held him close.

"It's okay, baby," she said, stroking his hair. "It's okay."

"I woke you up again. I'm sorry."

"It's all right. I'm a light sleeper anyway. Was it that same dream?"

He pulled away from her. "No," he said, frowning. "This one was different."

"What was it?"

"I was a soldier," he said. "I was walking guard duty on some farm in upstate New York. Watching a corn field. There was a girl . . . a very young girl, the foreman's daughter. She came out to the field, looking for me. We talked for a while, and then we started making love."

"Doesn't sound like too bad of a dream," said Raven, smiling.

"She died," said Steele. "She was kneeling on top of me, and someone shot her with a bow and arrow. The arrow came right through her chest. She fell down on me . . . there was blood everywhere. . . ."

"Jesus."

"Outlaw raiders," Steele said. "They were after the corn."

"What happened?"

"I don't know. I scrambled for my rifle and just as I got to it, I was hit." His hand went to his shoulder. "That's it. Then I woke up."

"That ever happen to you?" she asked.

Steele shook his head. "No. I was never in the army. I've never been to upstate New York. I've never even seen a corn field. But it happened to *someone*. And whoever he was, he must've lived through it, otherwise I wouldn't have the memory."

"You think it was that same person who was married to Donna and had the three kids?" asked Raven.

"No. It didn't feel the same. This was someone different. A young kid. The memory was much stronger." He took a deep breath and let it out slowly. "Christ, I've got fucking ghosts inside me. They're part of my goddamn mind."

Raven put her arms around him and pulled him close.

"What are you going to do?"

"I don't know," he said, holding her. "I just don't know. If I tell them, they'll put me down again and go into my brain . . . try to debug the program . . . I might not come out the same."

"Okay," she said, kissing him on the neck. "Okay, then we just won't tell them. I won't say a thing. We'll handle this together. We'll get through it. I'll be here for you, I promise."

He pulled away from her and looked into her eyes. For a moment, they simply stared at one another, then she leaned forward, put her hand on his cheek and gently kissed his lips. Once, twice, three times. The fourth time, he hugged her close and she moved up against him, slipping her tongue into his mouth.

He pulled her down onto the bed and they kissed hungrily, then her head moved down to his chest, her lips caressing him gently, her tongue flicking out to touch his nipples lightly. She moved down lower and Steele moaned softly as the tip of her tongue touched him and then her lips softly slid down over him. He pulled her around and buried his head between her long, slim legs. They lay locked together for a while, then she turned around and pulled him over on top of her. As he entered her, she gasped, looked up at him and softly said, "I love you."

And he believed it.

8

Tommy B wasn't taking any chances this time. He hated having to do it, because it was like admitting to a weakness, that he didn't trust himself to figure out how to do this job on his own, but he knew that Paulie wouldn't see it that way. When it came to anything outside running the complicated business aspects of the family, little Paulie was like part of the furniture, and he'd be thrilled to be consulted on something like this. It would make him feel important. And that was just how Paulie had reacted.

The day after Tommy came to him for help, stressing how very confidential it was, that it was a job the old man himself had wanted done and that he should not under any circumstances discuss it with anyone, Paulie called him and said, "I've got that information you wanted."

Tommy didn't waste any time getting down to Paulie's quarters on the first floor, in the west wing of the mansion. Although they lived separated only by two floors, Tommy hadn't been down to Paulie's rooms since they were kids. Even then, he thought, Paulie had been a wimp, more interested in reading and playing with his computers than in the games that he and Rick had played with the other kids in the enclave. The three brothers were as different as brothers could possibly be, except for a physical resemblance that was much stronger between Tommy and Rick than between them and Paulie. They were very much their father's sons, while Paulie took more after their mother. All through their early childhood, little Paulie had been Tommy's whipping boy, yet curiously, like a slavish dog that comes to lick its master's hand after it's been beaten, Paulie had never held it against him.

There had always been a sort of sibling rivalry between Paulie's older brothers, but it was more on the side of Tommy than of Rick. Tommy was the oldest one, expected to be stronger and better at their games, but it was Rick who usually came out on top, seemingly without much effort. And without any visible emotion, either. Rick was physically stronger, he was more athletic, he was quicker, and he always beat Tommy in any competition, though he was never smug about it, and it never seemed to make much difference to him that he had won. And it was that very nonchalance that drove Tommy crazy, and usually he took it out on Paulie.

Rick had never abused their little brother, but he never paid any attention to him, either, and though Paulie suffered from the torments that Tommy inflicted on him, it was almost as if he preferred that to being ignored, as Rick ignored him. And almost everybody else, for that matter. Paulie was a wimp, thought Tommy, but Rick . . . Rick was just plain spooky.

Paulie's room had not changed much since when he was a kid. If anything, it had become even more of a spilling cornucopia of books and tapes, computer terminals and various electronic gizmos. It looked like the inside of a space station, which was appropriate, Tommy thought, because Paulie was a real space cadet. He sat there in his room like some kind of mole, the old man's pet accountant, taking care of business and keeping tabs on various complex transactions, not caring one way or another about what they were concerned with. To him, it was just a symphony of numbers and data.

And when he wasn't doing that, he played with his computers, devising esoteric programs or entertaining himself with books from his voluminous collection of classic science fiction, most of it written years ago, before the Bio-War. Authors like Harlan Ellison and Norman Spinrad, William Gibson and Bruce Sterling, Orson Card, J.G. Ballard and Edward Bryant, all people Tommy'd never heard of. Once a month, Paulie would scuttle out from the confines of his room like some silverfish and have one of the men drive him down into the city, where he spent hours going from one used bookstore to another. He'd come back with a trunkload of the stuff that he kept piling up on his shelves until there was no room for any more and they'd start spilling over onto the tables, into boxes, in piles on the floor . . . it got so you could barely move in there. Tommy had tried looking at some of the stuff once, and he couldn't make head nor tail of it. Damn stuff made no sense. But Paulie treasured every single tattered, dog-eared copy.

He was sitting at one of his computers as Tommy came into his room, which had all the curtains drawn as usual. There was hardly any light, except for Paulie's desk lamp and the glow from the screens of half a dozen or more computer terminals. He sat there at his desk, as pale and ethereal as a ghost, looking almost like a girl with his soft, pretty features and his long dark hair falling to his slender shoulders. The old man usually disapproved of that and from time to time, he'd snap at one or another of the men to "get a fucking haircut," but this disapproval did not seem to extend to Paulie. Little Paulie could always get away with everything. But then Little Paulie never really did anything that he had to get away with, and he kept the family business running smoothly.

"What'cha got for me, Paulie?" Tommy said as he came into the darkened room.

"Take a look at this," said Paulie.

He punched up a full color graphic display on the computer. It was a model of a building.

"What the hell is that?" said Tommy. "I come to you for a plan and you show me a picture of some fuckin' building?"

"It's not just any building," Paulie said. He punched a couple of buttons on the keyboard and a cross-section of the building appeared. "It's a plan of the building where Steele lives. He's got the penthouse floor."

"Yeah? How the hell'd you get a hold of that?"

"City Housing and Planning Commission," Paulie said. "I just pulled it from their databank."

"No kiddin'? That's good, Paulie. That's good."

Paulie beamed at the praise. "Look here," he said. Little

red lights lit up all over sections of the building. "This is where they've got their security systems. And they've recently made some new additions. Those things up there on the penthouse roof are automated anti-aircraft gun turrets, controlled from the central security station inside the building. That's this blue area over here. These yellow lights represent video cameras. They've got the whole building pretty well covered. And they've got radar, too. That's the orange, up here. Short of taking out the entire building with a guided missile or something, there's just about no way to hit this place. At least, none that I can see."

"So why can't we use some kinda missile, like you said?"

"Because you'd kill a lot of other people, Tommy."

"So what?"

"So there's a lot of federal personnel living in this building," Paulie explained patiently. "Legislators, Congressional aides, bureaucratic employees—"

"So?"

"So some of them are on our payroll," Paulie said. "They're our people. And Papa's gone to a lot of trouble over the years to set up those connections. That's how we were able to hijack that weapons shipment. One of them tipped us off and got us all the information. And we've got other deals working through some of them. They're valuable."

"Can't any of them get us in?"

Paulie shook his head. "They'd blow their cover. Security's too tight in there. And even if you did get in, there's no way you'd ever get back out again."

"Yeah, all right," said Tommy wryly. "So what you're telling me is that all this shit comes to nothing but a big fat zero, right? So where's the plan, Paulie?"

"I'm getting to that," said Paulie. "Look here." He punched a few more buttons on the keyboard.

"What's that?"

"It's a subway terminal underneath the building," Paulie said. "There's a small shuttle train that runs directly from the Federal Building, strictly for the VIPs. Keeps them from having to brave the streets at night when they're having late sessions in Congress. And sometimes they just cut out and go back home to catch a few winks or have some dinner, spend some time with the family or whatever until they get called back for a roll call vote, so they need to shuttle back and forth quite often.''

"So what does that have to do with anything?'' asked Tommy, getting irritated. Fucking Paulie was wasting his time.

"I'll show you," Paulie said.

The picture scrolled across the screen, following the shuttle tunnel back toward the Federal Building, still in cross section, showing the tunnel and the buildings on the streets above it. Tommy had to give it to him, Paulie had gone to a lot of trouble to put all this together, but he still didn't see what any of it had to do with taking care of Steele. Then Paulie stopped it.

"Look here," he said, pointing at the screen.

"What's that?"

"It's another subway tunnel," Paulie said. "One of the old tunnels from before the war that they're not using anymore. There's no lines running through it. They've got it sealed off where the shuttle tunnel cuts through it, but I checked on it, and all they've got it sealed off with is heavy steel grates. You can get through those without a lot of trouble."

"What for?"

"So you can run something out on the tracks and block off the tunnel," Paulie said.

"Why the hell would I want to do that?"

Paulie gave him a patient look. "To stop the shuttle half-way down the tunnel," he said.

"Why?"

"Hostages, Tommy. You can't get into Steele's building. You can't hit his penthouse from the outside with choppers. You try to catch him going in or out, like you did before, and unless you manage to drop him right away, he's out in the open where he can maneuver, and he's got all the security inside the building for backup. And they'll be ready for something like that now. They'll probably have people posted on the rooftops all around the building and across the street. But if you can take a bunch of Congressmen as hostages, then you can get Steele to come to you, on ground that you can choose, and you can have him exactly where you want him. You get him to come out here on the Island, on roads where you can check to make sure he's not being followed by any backup units."

"Hey, Paulie, that's not bad," said Tommy. "That's not bad at all. Only how do we know when to hit the shuttle?"

"Easy," Paulie said, basking in his older brother's praise. "We have one of our people in the Federal Building tip us off. Somebody dependable, someone who's got an awful lot to lose if he screws up. I've already got the man in mind. Sanderson, the representative from New Jersey. He's the one who tipped us on that ordnance job, and he's got family that we can get to, but that probably won't be necessary. He's a wheeler dealer, sharp and very cool. Not the type to lose his nerve in a pinch, and he's into us real deep. We wait till Congress is having one of its late sessions and legislators have to be called back for a vote. We have Sanderson tip us off and make sure that he'll be on that shuttle."

"Yeah, okay," said Tommy, impressed. "Only what happens if we snatch some of the other people on our payroll?"

"That's part of the plan," said Paulie. "We'll need them later, but we won't tip them off in advance, just to play it safe. That way we make sure nobody loses their nerve at the last minute and misses that shuttle. Sanderson will be the only one who'll know what's going down. He's a take charge kind of guy. He can make sure everyone stays calm, tell them not to do anything stupid, just do what they're told. Cooperate with the kidnappers and not try any heroics. We simply make sure that nothing happens to any of our people. We segregate them from the others after we've made the snatch and stash them somewhere comfortable, on the theory that you don't want to keep all your hostages in one place, in case the feds should try anything. Then we can let them know what's going down."

"Yeah," said Tommy, nodding. Paulie had really thought this out. "Yeah, okay. All right. It's a good plan, Paulie. It's a real good plan."

"That's only part of it," said Paulie, smiling, thrilled that

Tommy approved. "Wait till you hear the rest. I've got the whole thing figured out, down to the last detail."

"Okay, so give," said Tommy, anxious to hear it all.

"Well, the first thing we have to do is make certain that none of this gets back to us," said Paulie. "Papa won't like it if it gets out that the family's kidnapped a bunch of Congressmen."

"Yeah, I hadn't thought of that," said Tommy, remembering what the old man had said to him. "So how do we get around that?"

"After you've taken care of Steele, you kill the hostages, except for Sanderson and the others we control, of course, and they'll be the only ones left alive to identify any of the kidnappers. When it's all over, they'll look through the files with the cops, and the only people they'll pick out as ones who were part of the gang will be Delano people. We can show them a few photographs and brief them so they'll know the right ones to pick out. The whole thing will be set up to look like the Delanos pulled it."

Tommy was impressed. Real impressed. He didn't think that Paulie had it in him to be this cold. But a possible flaw in the plan occurred to him.

"But if we whack all the others," he said, "how do we account for the ones who get out of it alive? What are they supposed to do, escape?"

"No," Paulie said, leaning back in his chair and smiling. "We rescue them."

"We *rescue* them?"

"Sure," said Paulie. "The hostages will be split up into two groups, remember? One of the groups will be the legislators on our payroll. The other group will be the ones we kill. When news of the kidnapping gets out, we call the media and make a big ransom demand. In the name of the Delanos, of course. Then we call Steele and tell him that if he wants to see the hostages released alive, he'll do exactly as we tell him. He'll know that it's a trap, but he won't have any choice. If we get accused of engineering the snatch, we issue a statement on behalf of Papa denying it, claiming it's a frame and promising that to prove it, the family will do everything in its power to assist the authorities in obtaining the return of the hostages. Then, after you've taken care of Steele, we send out some people to hit one of the Delano warehouses down on the south shore. Hit it hard, blow it up and make a lot of noise. Then we have Rick deliver Sanderson and the others to the police. We use Rick because he's immediate family, and he's got no warrants on him, so he can still go into the city. We alert the media, make sure they're on hand to get footage of Rick and some of our people bringing in the hostages. And Sanderson and the others will tell them that they were being held in that Delano warehouse that we hit and that Rick and his people rescued them. Rick will say we got a tip where the hostages were being held, but the Delanos killed off the others before we could get to them. And the Delanos will get the blame for whacking Steele as well. They'll scream like crazy and deny it, but no one will believe them. And the family will come out of the whole thing looking like the good guys and smelling like a rose.''

Tommy stared at his little brother with amazement. "Jesus Christ, Paulie, that's incredible. You're a fuckin' genius.''

"Thanks, Tommy,'' Paulie said, looking down at the floor shyly.

"You did good, Paulie. You did real good. I can't see where the plan could fail.''

"I worked on it real hard, Tommy. I'm glad you like it.''

"Yeah, yeah, I like it. Only look, there's a lot at stake here, you understand what I'm sayin'? And, if for some reason, anything should go wrong—not that I think it will—I just want to make sure that none of it comes down on you. I mean, if anybody screws up, you know, it won't be your fault, but whoever thought the plan up will probably get the blame, and the old man will hit the ceiling. I really appreciate all the help you've given me on this, and I want to show my appreciation, so I'll tell you what I'll do. I'll take the heat, okay? I'll say that I came up with the plan and that you just helped me work out some of the details. That way, just in case anything doesn't play the way it should, it'll all come down on me.''

"You don't have to do that, Tommy,'' Paulie said, looking

concerned. "I wouldn't want you to get into any trouble, not on account of me."

"Hey, we're brothers, right? Brothers are supposed to take care of each other. Besides, I can handle it. The old man won't be too hard on me. But you, this sort of thing isn't normally your business, know what I'm sayin'? The old man would think you had no call to get involved in putting together something like this when you've had no experience. I'll just say that the whole thing was my idea in the first place, that way you'll be covered, just in case."

"You'd do that for me?" Paulie said, wide-eyed. "Jeez, Tommy, thanks. I really appreciate it. I don't know what to say."

"No sweat, kid. But look, if it makes you feel any better, you can figure that you owe me one, okay?"

"Yeah, sure thing, Tommy. Anything you say. You name it It's really swell of you to do this."

"Hey, it's just my way of showing my gratitude," said Tommy magnanimously. "Come on, what do you say we have a drink?"

Oliver Higgins sat back in his office chair, smoking his pipe and listening to the tape-recorded conversation that took place between Dev Cooper and Phillip Gates in Cooper's apartment on Sutton Place. Neither of them suspected that he had both their homes bugged, as well as their phone lines, just as he had bugged everyone else who worked on the project. Including Steele.

Higgins suspected that Steele knew that they could tap into his electronic brain through the broadcast interface, but lately, he had resisted doing so. There hadn't been any real reason to. So far, Steele was performing up to expectations and doing the job he'd been sent out to do. Higgins didn't much care how he went about it, so long as he got it done, and he couldn't complain about the publicity that Steele was generating. For the first time, his superiors were starting to look with favor on the project, and there was talk of additional funds forthcoming that would enable them to undertake the next step in the plan. Things were going very well. But this new development with Gates and Cooper—Higgins wasn't quite sure what to think about that.

He had known for some time that Gates was sneaking classified material home with him, and he had done nothing to stop him, though he had him watched carefully. Gates was not the type to market classified material. He had no real ambition. Technically, he had compromised project security, but to date, no harm had come from it. He had simply taken some small pieces of equipment and some programs so that he could work with them at home. And with the security in his building, there was no chance of his place being burglarized. Gates was always careful, if a bit lax about security procedures, and it was no great problem to keep tabs on him. But Dev Cooper, that was another story.

Cooper was a bit too independent for Higgins' taste. And now he had just proven that he wasn't trustworthy. Not that trust was a commodity that Higgins ever dealt in. He did not believe in trust. He believed in information. Information was power. Information was control. Information was security. And, if Higgins had his way, to safeguard the security of the government, he would have placed a bug in every bedroom in the country. Cooper was, in effect, blackmailing Gates into withholding information. Information that could prove vital to the success or failure of the project. If Steele's personality was, indeed, in the process of fragmenting, he'd have to be pulled in and debugged before it became serious. No question about that. But Steele seemed to be okay, and Higgins was fascinated with what the two of them were doing. It had some extremely interesting implications.

"What do you want me to do about this?" asked Connors, the agency chief of project security. "You want me to bring them both in?"

"No," said Higgins thoughtfully. "Not just yet. Let's see what they do. I want you to keep close tabs on both of them. Maintain surveillance around the clock. And keep me posted on anything Gates takes out of the labs, any data he pulls from the project files. Keep an especially close eye on Cooper, but make sure he doesn't know he's being kept under surveillance. He's sharp, so tell your people not to be sloppy. I want to see where he goes with this.''

"Whatever you say," said Connors.

"What have you got for me on this girl, Raven?"

Connors consulted his notes. "Her real name's Ravenna Scarpetti," he said. "She's a hooker. Folks dead, no living relatives. She apparently came out of the Borodini enclave out on the Island. Tommy B took a personal interest in her when she was about fifteen or so. Tommy likes 'em young. He used to squire her around Midtown, take her to all the fancy joints he used to hang around in to rub shoulders with the in-crowd. Word is they had a lover's quarrel when she caught Tommy in the sack with one of her friends. She cut him and gave him that scar on his face. He apparently worked her over real good, then sold her to a pimp in no-man's-land, a psychopath named Rico who's part of the prostitution operation the Borodinis run. She's been with Rico ever since. She's had several arrests for assault and battery and assault with a deadly weapon, but the charges were all dropped.''

"Interesting," said Higgins, nodding. "So it all fits. Steele's using her as a source of information about the Borodini enclave. And undoubtedly for other things, besides," he added with a smile.

"You want to bring her in for questioning?"

"No, leave her alone. Just keep an eye on her. What about Ice?''

"He's another story," Connors said. "We've been trying to put something together on him ever since he came to us, but it's really hopeless. He was born in no-man's-land, so like most people out there, there isn't any record on him. Officially he doesn't exist. And all we really know about him is that he's big and black and he could probably eat this desk if he felt like it. We don't know his real name. We don't know how old he is. Prior to his coming to prominence as leader of the Skulls, absolutely nothing's known about him, and with what we've heard, we can't separate fact from rumor. He's been playing ball so far. When he isn't out with Steele, he keeps to himself in his room, except for that one time he went out to take the girl shopping for some clothes.''

"What does he do in there?" asked Higgins.

"Sleeps. Watches television. Reads."

"*Reads*? That neanderthal can read? What does he read, comic books?"

"Would you believe Dickens?"

Higgins stared at him. "You're joking."

"Square business," Connors said. "One of the security guards at the building takes night classes at the university and has a thing for the classics. Said Ice saw him reading a book one time while he was on break and asked him what it was about. Guy told him about it. It was *Tale of Two Cities*. Ice asked if he could borrow it when he was through. The man saw no harm, so he said sure. Ice has been borrowing books from him ever since. Dickens, Walter Scott, Robert Louis Stevenson. . . ."

"No kidding. Who would've thought it?" said Higgins. "There must be more to that gorilla than meets the eye."

"I've been thinking we could slip a mild sedative into his food," said Connors, "then give him a shot and wring him out. He wouldn't even know it, and it would give us some background on him."

"No," said Higgins. "I don't think there's really any need for that. At least, not yet. So long as he behaves himself and does what he's told, I really don't care who the hell he is. He's not that important." He shrugged. "What would we find out? That he was born in the ghetto, learned how to survive on the streets, started running with the gangs and working out until he got as big as a house and took over the Skulls? There's nothing there of any interest."

"We could find out everything he knows about the gang's operations," Connors said.

"Who cares?" said Higgins. "The gangs are of no interest to me. Let the police worry about them. I'm concerned with Borodini. He's the only one who's really powerful enough to pose a threat. With Borodini gone, the gangs will fall back to fighting among themselves again. My objective is for Steele to prove his worth by taking care of Borodini. Once he's done that, the committee will be falling all over themselves to get us the funding that we need."

"What if he fails?" said Connors.

"He won't fail," said Higgins. He smiled. "He's pro-grammed not to."

Dev Cooper looked in the mirror. He looked terrible. He looked like he hadn't slept in days. He also looked hung over. And he felt it, too. After Gates left he had tried to get some sleep, but it simply wouldn't come. His mind kept clicking over . . . like a computer, he thought. He couldn't turn it off. So he had decided to get drunk. For a man with his capacity for alcohol, that took some doing, but he managed. Eventually, he had passed out. He woke up at ten the next morning, his head bursting. He had called in sick. It really made no difference. In his position, he didn't have to punch a time clock. His hours were his own to designate, but he had called in just the same, to let them know he wasn't feeling well and wouldn't be coming in and to tell them he could be reached at home.

He felt exhausted. He felt like going back to bed and waiting until the hammering in his head went away. He opened up the medicine cabinet and took out the small bottle of pills he had prescribed for himself. Uppers. He shook a few out into his hand and stared at them. Not a wise thing to do to take them on a hangover, with the alcohol still in his system. Not a wise thing to take them at all. He took them anyway, washing them down with water.

He knew that he should probably eat something, but he couldn't stand the thought of food. He got into the shower and ran the water cold, as cold as he could stand it, and simply stood there, gasping and shivering as the water beat down on his body. He tried to will the headache away. He got out after a few minutes and dried himself off, then threw on his terry bathrobe and made a fresh pot of black coffee. He reached for the package of cigarettes on the kitchen table, shook one out and lit it. Booze, pills, coffee and cigarettes. Keep it up, Dev, he thought to himself, reach for every crutch that you can find. You're turning into a real manic.

He wished he had a therapist that he could talk to. Typical psychiatric daisy chain. Patient comes to a psychiatrist and unloads his problems, psychiatrist visits his psychiatrist to unload some of the stress and anxiety that the patient unloaded on him, that psychiatrist then goes and sees his *own* psychiatrist and so on down the line, one grand and endless game of broken telephone. I'm fucked up, pass it on. Only Dev had no psychiatrist he could go and talk to, because he couldn't talk about this case. It was all highly classified. . . . Well, he'd already shot that all to hell by bringing home the program, but even if he went to see another therapist, he didn't know what the hell he'd say.

"Doctor, I made a copy of a man, and I've got him trapped inside my personal computer. He thinks he's under mild sedation. Actually, since he's got an electronic brain, he thinks he's on downtime, but I don't know how long I can keep this up. He's starting to ask a lot of questions. I don't know what to tell him."

"Hmmm. Very interesting. And how long have you felt this way?"

Dev grimaced as he inhaled deeply and coughed. He wasn't used to smoking cigarettes, but he was getting accustomed to them fast. His eyes focused on the black liquid percolating in the coffeemaker. Plop, plop. Plop, plop. Like a heartbeat. He didn't even wait for the coffeemaker to finish percolating. As soon as the liquid looked dark enough, he poured himself a steaming cup.

It was a rotten thing he'd done to Phil Gates. He couldn't forget the look in the man's eyes, the way his face fell when he told him.

"You'd really do that?"

And Dev, hating himself, saying, "Try me."

"You son of a bitch. I thought you were my friend."

You son of a bitch. Said completely without bitterness or rancor. Stated flatly, like a fact. Yes, indeed, thought Dev, it was a fact. But then the other part . . . I thought you were my friend. The disappointment laced into that phrase. Disappointment that Dev, being who and what he was, had recognized instantly. The disappointment of a man who wasn't used to having friends, who, perhaps, did not have any real friends at all, only acquaintances and co-workers. The disappointment of a man who, deep down inside, did not *expect* to have any friends and was, in fact, prepared to be let down because it had happened to him so many times before. Disappointment that could probably be traced all the way back to his childhood, when he had been fat, awkward and ungainly—Dev could see the boy as he called to his mind the image of Phil Gates, the man—a clever boy, clever and highly intelligent, shy, socially awkward, his mind already enthralled with concepts his peers couldn't even begin to grasp. The boy who had forever been the outsider and the reject, an object of fun and perhaps torment, seeking refuge in the stimulation of his superior brain and gratification in food. It had been that boy who'd spoken to him. It had been his expression Dev had seen, the gruff facade of the sullen cybernetics engineer stripped away to reveal the insecure little boy within, the inner child that no one ever really loses.

"Damn it," Dev said. "Damn it!"

He threw the coffee cup against the wall and it shattered into sharp ceramic shards, splattering black coffee everywhere.

It didn't make him feel any better. But it was probably a healthy thing to do, thought Dev wryly. Don't repress it. Let it out. Okay, it's out. *Now* what?

"Shit."

Compulsively, he picked up a sponge from the kitchen sink and started wiping up the mess. After he had picked up all the pieces of the shattered coffee cup, certain he had missed some and that he'd find them when he walked on them barefoot, he got another cup of coffee and sat down at the kitchen table to drink it and smoke another cigarette. He looked through the doorway of the kitchen and into the other room, where the computer sat atop his desk like a malignant, electronic dwarf, its screen staring at him like a blind eye, not seeing him, but knowing he was there.

He swallowed hard and took a deep breath, trying to steady his nerves. It didn't work. He could feel the uppers starting to kick in, and he knew there was no going back to bed, no sitting there and feeling sorry for himself, no wallowing in guilt over his rotten treatment of Phil Gates, nothing for it but to go confront the specter or expend the drug-induced energy

in something utterly pointless, like a cleaning frenzy—the
apartment *could* use a thorough cleaning—but no, he pushed
that tempting thought aside. Even without the headache, which
he was either starting to get used to or the uppers were
making less noticeable or else, in his current masochistic
mood, he was starting to actually like it, it wouldn't work.
No matter where he went in the apartment, that computer's
blind CRT eye would follow him everywhere, reminding him
of the Steele program lying there dormant with its unan-
swered questions.

There was no avoiding it. This is why he was *here*, why he
had traveled halfway across the country to New York to
accept an opportunity most people in his field would have
killed for and which still fascinated him like nothing he had
ever done before, despite the fact that it was driving him to
drink and drugs. Despite the fact that it was starting to really
scare him. He went over to the computer and turned it on,
inhaled deeply, exhaled heavily, bit his lower lip, lit up yet
another cigarette with a trembling hand and booted up the
program.

"Steele?"

Steele's voice, or an electronic facsimile of it, issued from
the voice synthesizer peripheral. "That you, Dev?"

"Yes, it's me. How do you feel?"

"I don't."

The voice sounded edgy.

"You don't?"

Slow on the uptake. The moment he said it, he realized
what Steele . . . what the program meant.

"I don't feel *anything*. I can't feel my body. I can't see. I
can't move my arms or legs. I don't even feel like I'm
breathing."

"That's perfectly normal," Dev lied. "It's like I explained
to you before, you're not really fully conscious. Your bodily
functions are slowed down on downtime, and you're not
really aware of—"

"Why are you lying to me, Dev?"

Dev hesitated, taken aback by the response. "Why would I
lie to you?"

"I don't know. I can hear it in your voice. You're under a lot of stress."

Right, thought Dev. It's a computer programmed with human mental engrams. A cop's mental engrams. A cop's instincts. And a computer's ability to analyze vocal response patterns and identify a lie. Hadn't thought of that. Stupid, stupid. . . .

"I haven't been sleeping well lately," Dev said, hoping it would pass because it was the truth. He hadn't been. "And I got drunk last night and I'm hungover and I took some pills. . . ."

He stopped himself, aware that he was sounding manic. Fucking pills. He shouldn't have taken them.

"Why can't I see, Dev? Why can't I open my eyes? Why can't I move? Why can't I *feel* anything?"

"I already told you—"

"Tell me the truth, Dev."

"I'm telling you the truth—"

"You're lying to me. If I'm on downtime, how come I can speak and hear without any problems, but I can't do anything else? How come I don't *remember* going on downtime?"

"I don't know," Dev said, chewing on his lower lip. "I really don't know why you can't remember, Steele. But it's okay. There's nothing wrong. We've simply found a way . . . that is, Dr. Gates found a way to allow me to talk to you while you're on downtime so that I can—"

"Stop lying, Dev. Stop it! I can tell you're lying. I can hear it in your voice. I'm not on downtime, am I?"

Dev hesitated.

"*Am* I?"

Christ, he thought. Turn it off. Turn it off.

"What have you done to me, Dev? Tell me."

Dev closed his eyes. He tried to think. You were injured. We had to effect repairs. We've had some of your senses disconnected so that . . . no, no, it wouldn't work, he'd know. . . .

"What's happened to me, Dev? What's happened to my body?"

Jesus, Jesus. . . .

"Answer me, Dev."

Dev thought frantically. Can't lie to him anymore. He's learned to analyze my vocal responses like a fucking lie detector. What do I say? What the hell do I *say*?

"Where's my body, Dev? What have you done with it?"

Dev quickly quit the program and shut down the computer. He sat there, his hands trembling, his heart racing. He leaned his head back against the chair and closed his eyes. God help me, he thought. What have I done? What have I *done*?

9

The engineer who operated the shuttle that ran from the Federal Building to the government residential complex on Park Avenue always drove very carefully. His passengers were government employees and legislators, people with a considerable amount of clout. They wanted a smooth ride and didn't like being rattled around on the old tracks. A complaint could wind up costing him his job, so he made a habit of driving as if he were ferrying eggs. Consequently, he had plenty of time to brake when he saw the obstruction in the tunnel.

His first thought was that the old tunnel had collapsed, then he realized, as he drew closer, the shuttle slowing down with a squeal of pneumatic brakes, that someone had run one of the old subway maintenance carts out onto the track. For a moment, this puzzled him, as he knew that the intersecting side tunnel had been sealed off, but he wondered about it only for a moment. That was about all the time he had, because a man wearing a ski mask suddenly appeared on the tracks directly in front of him and emptied an automatic weapon directly into his window. The glass shattered into a thousand fragments as the bullets punched through it, smashing into the engineer's face and chest, throwing him back against the wall of his tiny operator's cubicle.

Another masked man leaped up onto the coupling between the cars, climbed over the chains and opened the door. He quickly made his way to the operator's cubicle, shoved the bloody body aside, and threw the lever that opened the passenger car doors.

The passengers looked up in fear and disbelief as ski-masked men carrying assault rifles and pistols climbed up through the doors. One man in each car fired a burst into the ceiling to make sure he had their complete and undivided attention. They each said more or less the same thing.

"All right, nobody move! Everybody does what they're told, nobody gets hurt!"

Congressman Julius K. Sanderson, the representative from New Jersey, was quick to respond to the situation.

"Okay, everybody, take it easy," he said to his shocked and frightened colleagues. "Just do *exactly* what they say. Please, don't anyone do anything foolish."

"Yeah, do like the man said," said Rick Borodini, through his ski mask. "Don't anybody do anything stupid."

They didn't need to be told twice. They meekly climbed down out of the shuttle cars and onto the tracks, then allowed themselves to be herded down the side tunnel by the gunmen. As Paulie had planned, it all went off without a hitch.

Working from the downloaded file he'd been fed from project headquarters and Raven's description of the mansion and its grounds, Steele had drawn a detailed plan of the Borodini enclave, which he laid out on the table for Ice and Raven to examine.

"The entire harbor's mined," said Steele. "If we came in by boat, we could detect the mines if we had the right equipment and moved slowly enough, but that would leave us sitting ducks for the patrol boats and the gun batteries on shore. And at night, they play searchlights out across the harbor. They'd let us come in about halfway, then simply blast us right out of the water."

"How about along the shore?" asked Ice.

"Same problem," Steele said, staring at the map. "The grounds of the estate are surrounded by minefields, and they've got intruder alarms and automated weapons emplacements. And the grounds are brightly illuminated at night. Same thing from the front. The only way in is up the front drive and it's all open. You've got minefields here and here, electrified gates, automated defense systems, armed perimeter guards with attack dogs, the works. And the estate itself is surrounded by the village that makes up the enclave. They've got armed guards with dogs patrolling the village streets, and there's not much chance of getting through the village without being seen by someone. And the village itself is surrounded by this wall here, which they've got covered every twenty-five yards or so by sentry towers. They've levelled the ground all around the outside of the wall. It's completely open and it's mined. There's only one way inside and that's by the main road, and they've got that covered six ways from Sunday."

"Shit," said Ice. "So how we get in there, then? Choppers?"

"Their surface-to-air missile batteries would take out any chopper before it got close enough."

"So you tellin' me there ain't no way to hit 'em?" said Ice.

"No, there's a way," said Steele. "We've got to get inside the mansion and shut down their defense systems, so Higgins can get his people in. Raven, that's where you come in. You're the only one who's actually been in there. We need to have a very detailed layout of the inside of the mansion. As much as you can remember."

"Only on one condition," she said. "I get to come along."

"We've been over that already," Steele said. "There's no way—"

"I can take care of myself, and I know my way around inside there," she said. "You want my help, you're gonna have to take me with you."

"Raven, look, I—"

"You think you're the only ones who've got a score to settle with the Borodinis?" she snapped. "I ain't gonna argue about it. Yes or no? What's it gonna be?"

The phone rang. Steele picked it up.

"Steele," he said.

"Hello, scumbag. This is Tommy Borodini," said the voice on the other end.

"How'd you get this number?"

"Shut up and listen. Turn on channel 7. I'll call you right back."

The line went dead.

Steele hung up the phone.

"Who was that?" asked Raven.

"Tommy B," Steele said. He turned on the TV.

"—on their way back to Congress for a roll call vote when they were abducted by an unknown number of armed men. The kidnappers apparently broke through one of the steel grates sealing off the tracks running from Government House to the Federal Building and gained access through one of the old, abandoned subway tunnels, through which they spirited the kidnap victims after they blocked off the tracks and killed the shuttle operator. At this moment, we do not yet know which members of the legislature or what other federal employees were among the kidnap victims, but we expect to have that information for you momentarily.

"A short while ago, this station received a call from a man who identified himself as a member of the Delano family, claiming credit for the kidnapping and demanding a ransom for the victims in the amount of ten million dollars. Terms of payment were not specified, and we are awaiting further word. Meanwhile, when reached for comment at his family's enclave in Brooklyn, Anthony Delano vehemently denied any knowledge of the kidnapping and claimed that someone was trying to frame him. We have had, as yet, no official statement from the authorities. For further details, we now go to Linda Tellerman, standing by at the Federal Building."

"Bob, when news of the abduction reached the chambers of Congress, the reaction here was shock and disbelief. The sheer audacity of this kidnapping has taken everyone here by—"

The telephone rang once more. Steele snatched it up.

"Yeah?"

"Listen carefully, 'cause I'm not gonna repeat myself," said Tommy B. "If you want to see any of those people alive again, you'll do exactly as I say."

"If you think you're going to get away with this," said Steele, "you must be out of your damn mind."

"Shut the fuck up and listen! Your place is bein' watched. You so much as make one move that I don't tell you to make, and all those people are gonna get iced. You listenin'?"

"I'm listening," said Steele tensely.

"You've got exactly one hour to get up the money. At that time—"

"There's no way anyone can get together ten million dollars in just an hour," Steele said. "You've got to give me more time."

"Don't hand me that. You just get it there or those people are dead meat. One hour. That's all you've got. Have it delivered to your place. I'll call you back at that time with further instructions. If it ain't there by then, or if I hear anything on the news about the Borodini family bein' behind this instead of the Delanos, you can kiss 'em goodbye."

He hung up the phone.

Steele immediately dialed Higgins.

"This is Steele. I need to talk to Higgins right away. It's an emergency."

He waited just a moment, then Higgins got on the line.

"Steele? I was just about to call you. You've heard about the kidnapping?"

"Yeah, I heard. Tommy B just called me. He's the one who pulled it off, not the Delanos. He wants the ten million ready in an hour, and I'm supposed to be the bagman. I've got to sit tight until the money gets here. He's having my place watched. He wants the money delivered to me here. He said if it's not here when he calls back with further instructions, or if word gets out that he's behind this and not the Delanos, he's going to kill the hostages."

"I see," said Higgins. "Okay, how do you want to handle this?"

"Can you get the money?"

"I can get it. He could have held us up for a lot more than ten million. You realize it's you he's really after? The money's only icing on the cake."

"I know. Have it delivered to my place by X-wing chopper," Steele said. "Get hold of somebody approximately my physical type, somebody who can pass for me at a distance. Have him armed and dressed in Strike Force riot gear. Get hold of Gates and have him wire a voice synthesizer into the helmet mike, programmed to sound like me. And have him hook up another one that can be slipped in place over a telephone receiver. Then have the guy come out here on the chopper. The chopper's going to drop him and the money off and pick us up. And I want you to get some scuba gear for me on that chopper as well. Can you do all that in an hour?''

"I'll manage," Higgins said. "What's your plan?''

"Tommy B's probably figuring on running me around for a while, to make sure I'm not being followed. I'm counting on that to buy us some time. Once he's got the money, those hostages are dead, so I figure our only chance is to grab a hostage of our own and force him to make a swap. We're going to hit the enclave and snatch Victor Borodini.''

"Think you can pull it off?''

"I'll have to. Have an assault unit standing by with choppers within striking distance of the enclave. I'll keep in touch by broadcast link. The moment we've got their defense systems neutralized, I'll give you the signal to hit the enclave. Have you got all that?''

"I'm on it," Higgins said.

Steele hung up the phone.

"Okay," he said, turning to Ice and Raven. "They've forced our hand, and we haven't got much time, so listen carefully. Here's what we're going to do. . . .''

As the chopper touched down on the penthouse helipad, they ducked down low and ran out to meet it. The man carrying the money got out of the hatch, dressed in full Strike Force riot gear.

"Agent Sharp, reporting as ordered," he said. The voice that came from the helmet's speaker was Steele's own. "Do I sound all right?''

"You'll do," said Steele. "I hope. You've got the phone hook-up?''

"Right here." He tapped his pocket.

"Good." Steele glanced at his watch. "Borodini should be calling in about ten minutes from now, unless he jumps the gun. He's probably going to run you, but if it looks like you're running out of time or if he tumbles to it, get onto Higgins right away.''

"Got it."

"And Sharp . . . watch yourself. At some point, he's going to run you right into a set-up for an ambush. Don't be a hero. Don't try to buy us time. If you smell anything wrong, get out of there and call Higgins right away."

"Will do. Good luck."

"You, too."

They got into the chopper and lifted off. Steele immediately started stripping off his clothes. Ice and Raven watched with fascination as he loaded his built-in weapons through the magazine ports in his arms. He then slipped into the wetsuit and zipped it up, then strapped on the pouch containing the special belt designed for carrying his accessory hands. It had thick, specially built nysteel discs attached to it, with locking mechanisms similar to those on his wrists sticking out from them and pointing downward, giving the belt the appearance of being studded with strange-looking metal conchas. He reached into his pack and started to attach the accessory hands to the belt, snapping them into the locking discs so that he could remove them again with a quick twist. The effect was surreal. He slipped the belt back into the pouch and tucked his .45, his knife, and black fatigues and boots in on top of it.

The X-wing chopper headed out toward the north shore of Long Island, flying very low over the water, the waves practically licking at its underside as it skimmed over Long Island Sound. Its turbine NOTAR system substituted an internal blower for the old, exposed tail rotor blade design, and it was constructed of epoxy-impregnated fiberglass, graphite and Kevlar, as strong as metal, but a fraction of the weight. Its X-wing design gave it a sleek, aerodynamic, teardrop shape, and it could hover, take off and land vertically using its helicopter-style rotor, but once in flight and moving at 200 mph, the four-bladed, graphite-fiber composite rotor blades stopped and locked into position, functioning as a fixed, X-shaped wing, turning the chopper into a jet and enabling it to approach the speed of sound.

The pilot, his head completely encased in his VCASS helmet, monitored the graphic displays fed to him by the Visually Coupled Airborne Systems Simulator, his computer-enhanced vision giving him much more information and affording far better "visibility" than was possible with the naked eye or conventional instrumentation. The X-wing chopper knifed its way over the water, sweeping around Sand's Point and hurtling towards Centre Island.

Both Ice and Raven were dressed in black Strike Force fatigues with riot helmets and body armor. They were not carrying the computer backpacks with integral missile launchers, into which the helmets were normally hooked, as there had been no time to train them in their use. The helmets, by themselves, would afford them some protection, as well as give them night vision and enable them to communicate with one another. For weapons, they carried the 4.7 mm., laser-sighted, caseless battle rifles, with select fire systems capable of semiautomatic, three-round burst or full auto; 9 mm. machine pistols and hand grenades in both fragmentation and incendiary. They carried spare magazine pouches on their belts and shoulder harnesses.

Use of those weapons was not complicated, and Steele had checked them out as best he could in the limited time they had available. Ice already had experience with automatic weapons from his days as leader of the Skulls, and he had used the Strike Force battle rifle once before, when he and Steele hit the warehouse. Raven, however, had never fired an automatic weapon, and Steele had spent most of the time they had in teaching her the use of both the battle rifle and the machine pistol. Now, in the chopper, Steele took advantage of the time to give her some practice with live ammo, firing out over the water through the open hatch.

"You'll see that it has practically no recoil," he said. "The high-velocity caseless ammunition is completely consumed on firing, and the weapon's gas-vented, so you won't have any brass flying around. There won't be any kick and there's no reason to flinch. It recoils much less than a conventional pistol. Don't worry about semiautomatic fire or three-round burst. Just leave it on full auto, hold it the way I showed you, and spray your target. Go ahead, try it."

Raven fired several bursts through the open hatch.

"No, like this," said Steele, taking the weapon from her

and demonstrating. "Sweep across your target. Here, try it again."

She squeezed off two more bursts. "Like that?"

"Yeah, like that," said Steele, nodding.

She picked up on it quickly, but he was still worried about how she'd do in actual combat. He didn't think much of her chances, but it was her decision. And after what Tommy B had done to her, she had a right to be there.

"Just remember to stick close to Ice and concentrate on letting him take out anyone in front of you," he said. "You just watch his back. And try not to shoot him."

"Yeah, I'd appreciate that," said Ice.

Raven grimaced at them.

"Okay," said Steele. "Let's do some live ammo work with the machine pistol."

As she unholstered the machine pistol and checked the magazine, just the way he'd shown her, he wondered how well Sharp was doing. He sincerely hoped that Tommy B was taking full advantage of the situation and enjoying himself while he ran Sharp all over town. They'd need all the time they could get. He could only hope Sharp wouldn't get blown before they hit the mansion. Or that Tommy B would not run out of patience.

The first contact had gone well. Tommy Borodini had called the moment the chopper took off from the penthouse helipad. Sharp picked up the phone and quickly slipped the synthesizer adapter Gates had given him over the receiver.

"Steele," he said.

"That chopper bring the money?" Tommy B snapped.

"Yeah. I've got it here."

"Good boy. Now listen carefully, I ain't gonna say this twice. You've got fifteen minutes to make it down to Third and 23rd. There's a phone booth on the corner. It's gonna ring four times. You don't pick it up by the fourth ring, the hostages are dead. Time starts right now. Get movin'."

Sharp hung up the phone, pulled on his helmet, snatched up the bag containing the money and ran for the elevator, which the building security guards had standing by so he wouldn't have to wait for it. The moment the doors opened on the lobby floor, he sprinted out to the Strike Force patrol unit warmed up and waiting for him at the curb. He threw the bag inside and shifted into gear, powering down the street for a straight run down to 23rd. Street. As he drove, he reached for the radio handset.

"Bagman to HQ," he said, avoiding using his own name despite the fact that he was on the scrambler circuit. He was Steele. No point in taking any chances of slipping up later by using his own name.

"HQ to Bagman, we read you. Go ahead."

"First contact made. I'm heading down to Third and 23rd. for second contact at a phone booth on the corner. I've got fifteen minutes. Keep the road clear."

"Will do."

"Bagman out."

The armored unit built up speed as it jounced over the potholes, siren blaring. So far so good, thought Sharp. Come on, Tommy, be a prick. Run me ragged. Make me work for it. We need the goddamn time.

The X-wing chopper slowed down and hovered low over the water, mere feet above the Sound. They were about five hundred yards offshore, just around the bend of the northwest point of the harbor.

"Okay," said Steele, "if everything goes according to plan, I'll give you the signal the moment I've got their defense systems shut down and their missile batteries out of commission. Then get in there fast with the assault unit and hit them hard. Remember, I don't want any choppers firing on the mansion. We need Borodini alive. Ice, you make sure they understand that."

"I got it," Ice said. "Good luck, man."

"Thanks."

Raven came up to him quickly and gave him a fierce kiss.

"Give 'em hell, Steele," she said.

"You just be careful," Steele said. "Don't get carried away when it goes down. Remember what I told you."

"I will."

He nodded, slipped the facemask over his head and dropped down through the hatch.

The chopper turned and started flying back to rendezvous with the assault force as soon as Steele hit the water. There was no need for a weight belt. The weight of his nysteel prosthetics made him start sinking at once. He slipped the breather into his mouth and started swimming underwater, propelling himself faster and faster with strong kicks of his powerful nysteel legs, cutting through the water like a shark. He switched in his thermal imager and infrared. He had a long swim ahead of him, and it would take him through a harbor full of mines, patrolled by gunboats that could be equipped with sonar that would pick him up if they came anywhere near him. He turned his hearing up full, listening for the sound of engines. So far, so good, he thought. If only Tommy B gave him enough time. . . .

_10_

Sharp made it to the corner of Third and 23rd. with time to spare. He leaped out of the patrol unit and ran over to the phone, carrying the bag with the money in his hand. They weren't taking any chances. The bag really contained ten million dollars in neatly packaged large bills. Sharp felt nervous carrying all that money. Once again, he checked his sidearm, a 10 mm. polymer/ceramic semiauto tucked into a shoulder holster. He also carried a small 9 mm. squeeze-cocking backup piece strapped in an ankle holster, a commando knife in a spring-loaded sheath strapped to his forearm, and a tiny .380 semiautomatic, small enough to fit in the palm of his hand, tucked into his shorts at the crotch, where he felt reasonably confident it would escape a frisk.

He glanced at his watch. Thirty seconds to go. He took out the telephone adapter and held it ready. When the phone rang, he picked it up on the first ring, quickly slipping the synthesizer adapter into place over the receiver.

"Steele," he said.

"Good," said Tommy B. "You're right on time. Let's see if you can keep it that way. Corner of 14th. and 8th. Five minutes."

Click.

Sharp ran quickly to the car and leaped inside. He laid rubber as he peeled out, heading south on Third Avenue down to 14th. Street. He was heading deep into no-man's-land. As he drove, he left the civilized part of the city behind and headed into darkness. There were no streetlights down here. The high beams of his armored patrol unit cut through the darkness, illuminating shabby-looking people who scurried back into the shadows as he passed. He reached 14th. Street and turned right, heading west towards 8th. Avenue, the unit careening around the craters in the street, lights flashing off the ruined buildings.

He could see fires burning in many of them, the only illumination and the only source of heat for the desperate people living down here. All too often, these old buildings caught fire, and no fire department ever came to put out the flames. Sometimes the residents managed to put out the fires themselves. More often than not, the buildings simply burned, and then, when the flames had finally gone out, if anything was left, the people moved back into the blackened ruins, preferring a charred environment they knew to a new abandoned building that could conceal unknown terrors far greater than the flames.

The car screeched around the corner of 14th. and 8th. and he pulled over to the curb. There was no telephone booth in sight. He didn't know why he should have expected one. There was no phone service in no-man's-land. There were no services of any kind except those provided by the gangs. He sat in his unit, the engine rumbling, wondering how contact would be made. He took out his pistol, thumbed the safety down and held it in his lap. Nervously, he rolled down the window.

He almost jumped when a voice said, "Avenue D and Houston. Move it. You got three minutes."

He heard the sound of running footsteps and realized that someone had crept up to the side of his vehicle while he was pulled over. His heart was pounding. Whoever it was could just as easily have lobbed a grenade in through his window.

He didn't waste any time. The car shot off down 8th. Avenue and he turned off on Greenwich, heading down to 6th., once known as the Avenue of the Americas. He opened it up all the way, flying over the buckled, cratered street. He turned left on Houston and headed east, across the island, to Avenue D down by the East River. He glanced at his watch. Cutting it close. The time was almost up. He made it to

Avenue D and pulled over to the side. There wasn't a sound except the loud idling of his engine. The streets were completely deserted. It was like a ghost town. He glanced at his watch. He was late. Shit. Shit. . . .

Something hit the side of his car. He snatched his pistol up and waited for the sound of the explosion, but it didn't come. He took a deep breath and cautiously opened the door. A brick was lying in the street beside his car with a note wrapped around it. He quickly picked it up, closed the door, and read the note.

"Corner of First and 34th.," it said. "Phone on corner. Four minutes."

"Christ," said Sharp, wrenching the shift lever into gear and peeling out, heading north on Avenue D, back up to 14th. Borodini was running him around in circles.

"That's okay, Tommy," Sharp said to himself as he fought the wheel. "Keep it up, you son of a bitch. Just keep it up. I've got all night."

For an ordinary man, the swim would have been an exhausting one, but for Steele, it was no more difficult than doing easy laps in a pool, which he had done in training to get accustomed to how his nysteel prosthetics performed in water. They performed well enough to break every existing swimming record. His powerful nysteel legs propelled him through the water as if he were a dolphin. He was well into the harbor before he encountered the first of the mines, but he had no difficulty in avoiding them. They were firmly anchored to the bed of the harbor, floating a few feet below the surface, aimed at taking out boats, not frogmen. With his bionic optics, Steele had no difficulty seeing in the water, and he swam easily between the moorings of the mines.

In the distance, his amplified hearing picked up the sound of a patrol boat's engines, and he angled out away from it, heading in toward shore. The boat did not change course; not surprising, since it would have run into the underwater mines if it had. Steele smiled around his mouthpiece. The very mines that were meant to protect the harbor from intruders were now protecting him.

He was using rebreather tanks so that no telltale bubbles would appear on the surface, giving him away. But he doubted that the patrol boats would expect one man to try swimming underwater the length of the entire harbor, which was about three miles from the tip of Centre Island to its southernmost end, only to face the formidable security on the grounds of the estate. This would be the easy part. The hard part would come when he came ashore.

Before long, the upward sloping bottom alerted him that he was getting in close to shore, and he cautiously broke the surface of the water, looking all around him. The mansion was about three hundred yards off to his right, on a gently sloping rise over the harbor. He could see the docks about a hundred and fifty yards off to his right. One of the patrol boats was tied up there, and several men, all armed with automatic assault rifles, were gathered around it on the dock. He heard their laughter as they killed some time together smoking cigarettes.

He scrambled up out of the water and plunged into some undergrowth near the water's edge, where he stripped off his wetsuit and tanks and hid them in the bushes. He opened up the waterproof pouch, took out his fatigues and boots and quickly put them on. Then he strapped on the belt containing his accessory "hands." He took out his father's old .45 Colt and tucked it into his waistband at the small of his back. He slipped the commando knife into its sheath. Then he started moving through the trees, heading uphill and toward the mansion.

He heard the dog a second before it sensed his presence. Even as it tensed, prepared to bark, the barrel of his dart launcher slid out through the port in his hand and fired. The dart whistled through the air and struck the animal, its poisoned tip killing it instantly. The second dart struck the guard in the chest before he even had time to react. Steele retracted the dart launcher and ran out quickly, staying low, and grabbed the body of the dog with one hand and the guard with the other and dragged them back into the trees. He could see the shore batteries halfway up the hill between the docks and the mansion, but he wasn't going to worry about those now. It was the automated defense systems he was concerned about, especially the surface-to-air missiles. The attack would have no chance of succeeding unless he could neutralize those, and for that he had to get inside the mansion.

The power lines from the plant in the village ran down to the main terminal in the basement, where, according to Raven, the auxiliary generators were also located. She said they'd had a blackout once and the generators had kicked in automatically within sixty seconds. He'd have to put them out of commission. That would leave the people in the control room unable to activate the defense systems, and the missiles would be useless. But the only way into the basement was through the first floor of the mansion.

There was a side entrance at the east wing on the first floor that led into a lounge area for the guards, just off the kitchen. That was where the video display monitors for the security cameras were. Raven said the guards held poker games and hardly ever paid attention to them. He sincerely hoped so. A hallway off the lounge led into the mansion, and the door to the basement stairs was off that hallway. If he could cut the power line from outside, that would leave him sixty seconds to get through the guardroom and past any guards who were in there, down the hallway, through the door to the basement and to the auxiliary generators. That was not a lot of time.

Steele hoped that they were standing by on the broadcast link. "Higgins," he thought. "Are you there?"

He "heard" Higgins' voice inside his mind. *"I'm here, Steele. Where are you?"*

"I'm on the grounds of the estate," he said, then realized that he had spoken out loud. Higgins "heard" him just the same.

"How does it look?"

"So far, so good," Steele said, still speaking out loud, but very softly. It seemed somehow more comfortable that way. "I've had to kill one guard so far, but I haven't set off any alarms. I've got to get in close to the mansion and cut the power lines. That'll leave me exactly one minute to get inside and knock out the auxiliary generators before they kick in. I'll let you know the minute I've got the lines cut, then stand by to give the signal for the choppers to move in. With any luck, you'll get it in about a minute. If you don't hear from me within five minutes after I go in, that'll mean I blew it.''

"Okay. We'll stand by for your signal."

Steele grimaced. It felt decidedly uncomfortable to have Higgins in his head, but he had to admit that, this time at any rate, it was certainly convenient. He wondered if Higgins had spent any time tiptoeing through his mind when he wasn't aware of it. He recalled the time he'd asked Susan Carmody about the backup copy of his program that he knew they had on file somewhere in their databanks. It was a conversation he was not likely to forget. In fact, unless something went wrong with his cybernetic brain, he would never forget anything ever again. He could recall the entire conversation word for word.

"Where is that file, Susan? You know where it is. You can get access to it."

"No, I couldn't. . . ."

"I want you to erase it for me."

"I can't. . . ."

"Why? You think it would be murder?"

"You . . . you don't understand. If anything should happen to you, it would be the only thing that could—"

"Something did *happen to me, Susan. I should've died. But thanks to that implant in my brain, you made yourself a backup copy of my soul and programmed it into a machine. Nobody's got the right to do that."*

"Steele, don't. . . ."

"I can find a way to live with what I am, whatever in hell that is, but I don't want to keep coming back again and again, just to keep your little experiment going. The next time I die, I want it to be for keeps."

"But you didn't *die!"*

"The way I was, I wouldn't call it living. And I'm not sure the way I am is, either."

"You don't understand. Don't you see? It would make no difference. Even if I could do as you ask, it would be discovered almost immediately, and Higgins could simply pull another data engram copy directly from you."

"Not if I can help it."

"You wouldn't even know it."

That was how he had discovered what he had already suspected, that they could tap into his mind. Access it through the broadcast link, just like they could access a computer program—which was exactly what he was. He wondered what would happen if he bought it on this mission. Would Higgins find himself another vegetable in some hospital somewhere, someone whose brain had been irreparably damaged so that they could have him declared legally dead and keep his body on life support while they took out his organic brain and implanted a cybernetic one into his skull, to be programmed with the backup copy of the Steele program? Would "he" suddenly wake up in a brand new body, with no memory of his death?

The thought of his dormant "alternate self" residing somewhere in the project databanks was something that haunted Steele, something that frightened him almost as much as the electronic "ghosts" lurking somewhere in his program. He had not told Higgins, Gates or Dev Cooper about them, but he wondered if they knew just the same. And if they knew, if they *could* read his mind, why hadn't they said or done anything about it? Were they simply waiting to see what would happen? Or was there a limit to what they could read in his mental engrams?

Steele pushed the thought aside. Now was not the time to agonize over those dilemmas. After this was over, there'd be plenty of time to try and sort things out somehow. And if he did not survive the next few minutes, then perhaps his problems would be over. Perhaps.

On the other hand, perhaps not.

He watched two of the guards coming up from the docks and circling around the back of the house, heading toward the side entrance where their lounge was. He took careful note of the path they followed. Intelligence had indicated that sections of the grounds around the estate were mined, and Raven had confirmed this, but she had also come up with a piece of useful information that intelligence didn't have on file.

There were pieces of slate set into the lawn at intervals of

about two feet, running in parallel about three yards apart,
forming a walkway that effectively indicated the proper paths
to take in order to avoid the areas that were mined. There
were no children at the estate, and the dogs did not run loose,
but there had been one occasion, Raven said, when an inebri-
ated guest had wandered out into the backyard and blown
himself to kingdom come. It had put a considerable damper
on the party. Consequently, Victor Borodini had ordered that
the mines be set back farther from the house, beyond a
waist-high hedgerow so that guests could walk in safety anywhere inside that landscaped perimeter. Beyond it, if one
wanted to get down to the shore or to the docks, it was
necessary to keep to the paths.

Raven had not known how many mines there were or
where they had been placed. And from where Steele watched
in concealment, he could not see the paths. Judging by where
the guards were walking, he would have to cover some
twenty-five to thirty yards before he could reach them. And it
was all well-lighted, open ground.

He also noticed that as the guards coming up from the
docks approached the house, two relief guards came out of
the lounge and started heading down to meet them. That
meant they were working shifts and one of the shifts was
changing. Which meant that it would not be long before the
guard he'd killed would be discovered missing. He didn't
have much time.

He reached down to his belt and unsnapped one of his
accessory "hands" from its locking disc. It did not resemble
a hand at all. It looked more like a short nysteel tube the same
diameter as his wrist, finished in matte black, about four
inches long, with six short turrets of varying diameters extending from it in a circle like the barrels of a miniature
Gatling gun. It would fit on either his right or left wrist, and
in the center, between the turrets, was a port through which
he could fire either his built-in dart launcher or the 10 mm. It
contained a built-in, miniaturized Geiger counter, a voltmeter
with the test cables retracted inside one of the small turrets,
and a metal detector, all of which fed their readouts directly
to his brain. He tucked the appendage underneath his left

arm, then released the lock on his left hand and snapped it in place on the belt. He took the "Swiss Army knife," as he thought of it, in his right hand and snapped it in place onto his left wrist. It locked in with a soft click.

About thirty yards of well-lighted, open ground to cover before he reached the hedgerow that marked the end of the minefield, and then he had another space of open ground to cover before he reached the house. He'd have to keep his eyes out for the guards and hope that no one would spot him on the monitors or from the back windows of the mansion. The barrel of the 10 mm. pistol built into his forearm slid out of the gunport in his right hand. He clicked it into the silencer attached to his belt, then held up his left hand with the turret attachments. It whirred softly as it revolved around, clicking the adjustable wrench into position. He put it over the silencer and it tightened down, then revolved quickly like a power screwdriver, screwing the silencer into place.

The guards heading back toward the house had now reached the side entrance. The ones heading down toward the docks were below him now, farther down the slope. If they didn't turn around and glance behind them, and if no one saw him on the monitors or through the windows of the mansion, and if none of the other guards came out, especially the ones with dogs. . . . Steele took a deep breath and crouched down low, holding his left arm out before him.

Well, here goes nothing, he thought, and started out across the lawn.

The phone was already ringing when Sharp reached it. He snatched up the receiver.

"Hello," he said breathlessly.

"Who the hell *is* this?"

Sharp froze. In his anxiety to get to the phone, he had forgotten to slip the adapter over the receiver. Thinking fast, he quickly slipped the adapter into place and held it well away from his mouth, saying loudly, "Get away from that phone!"

Then he held the phone up to his ear and said, "Borodini?"

"Who the hell was that? What's going on?"

"Just some guy standing on the street—picked up the phone before I could get to it."

Silence.

"Borodini?"

"Yeah, yeah, I'm here. Okay. Take the Midtown Tunnel to the Island. Follow the expressway out to the Meadowbrook Parkway. Head south to the coliseum. I'm givin' you half an hour to make it, so don't waste any time. You'll be watched at points along the way, you won't know where. If anyone's on your tail, the hostages are dead. Understand?"

"I understand," said Sharp. "I'll be alone."

"You better be."

"What do I do when I reach the coliseum?"

"Drive your car inside through the service bays and park in the center of the arena. Be sure to bring the money."

Borodini hung up the phone.

Well, this was it, thought Sharp, as he headed back toward the car. The Nassau Coliseum would be the last stop. The perfect place for an ambush. Steele had less than half an hour left to pull off the assault on the enclave and get Victor Borodini. As he pulled away from the curb, he reached for the handset.

"Bagman to HQ."

"HQ here. Go ahead, Bagman."

"I'm heading north on First Avenue to the Midtown Tunnel, then I'm taking the Long Island Expressway to the Meadowbrook Parkway and south to the Nassau Coliseum. It's going to go down there. I've got half an hour to make it. Any instructions?"

"Proceed as directed, Bagman. Keep us advised."

"Roger. Bagman out."

Proceed as directed. That meant the assault had not gone down yet. He bit his lower lip. Come on, Steele, he thought desperately. We're running out of time.

Steele moved quickly across the lawn, keeping low, running in serpentine around the buried mines. With his detector feeding the information directly to his brain, he could move much faster than a man working an ordinary metal detector,

and he could keep his eyes out for the guards. His cybernetic
brain analyzed incoming data far more quickly than a human
brain could and gave him reaction time far greater than that of
an ordinary man, so he was able to sprint across the minefield, instantly changing direction to avoid the mines like a
superhuman broken field runner. So far, no alarm.

He was halfway to the hedgerow when two guards appeared from around the other side of the house, seventy-five
yards away. One of them had a Doberman on a leash. He was
completely out in the open, and they couldn't avoid seeing
him. He saw the dog's ears prick up as he switched on his
laser designator, his eyes lighting up with two bright red
pinpoints as he brought his right hand up. The silenced pistol
coughed softly as he fired three shots in rapid succession. The
flat trajectory of the high-velocity 10 mm. jacketed hollowpoint
gave him the range to make all three shots count. The first
one hit the dog, dropping it in its tracks before it could start
barking. The second and third struck the two guards, both
head shots, killing them instantly.

Steele quickly looked over his shoulder toward the docks.
The other two guards hadn't heard. They were still walking
with their backs to him, talking to each other, oblivious to
what had happened behind them. Steele was thankful they
didn't have a dog. No alarm came from the mansion, but
there was no way to get over to where the two guards and
their dog had fallen and drag their bodies out of sight. They
would be exposed now and sure to be discovered within
moments. He wasted no time in zigzagging through the minefield and reaching the hedgerow. He vaulted it and sprinted
toward the side entrance of the house. As he ran, he retracted
his 10 mm. gun barrel back into his forearm and pulled out
the silenced Colt. In the close confines of the guard lounge,
he wanted the close-range knockdown power of the slower
bullet, without risk of overpenetration that could result in a
slug going through a wall and alerting someone on the other
side or needlessly injuring any of the household staff.

As he rounded the corner of the mansion, he ran right into
a guard coming around from the front, heading toward the
side entrance to the lounge. As the startled man gaped in

amazement, Steele quickly raised his turret attachment and shot him with a dart. The man crumpled to the ground without a sound. Steele quickly found the junction box where the power lines entered the house. The turret attachment on his left wrist revolved with a soft whirring sound and clicked into position. Another soft, brief whine of the miniature servo motor and the wire cutter extended from the turret. Steele tucked the .45 into his waistband, ripped open the cover of the box, reached in with the cutter and snipped the lines. There was a brief sparking and all the lights inside the mansion went out, simultaneously with the floodlights illuminating the grounds.

"Okay, Higgins, I'm going in! Time!"

Sixty seconds. The clock was running.

Steele switched in his thermal imagining system and ran for the side entrance. He could hear the guards inside, reacting to the sudden blackout. He threw open the door, drawing his Colt as he burst through into the darkened lounge. In a flash of perception, he could make out the thermal images of nine guards around the lounge, five of them sitting at a table, one by the coffeemaker, another standing by the refrigerator, two sitting in front of a television set. No one had been watching the video monitors.

The two in front of the suddenly dark TV screen were already on their feet and turning, the one by the refrigerator stood with his hand on the open door, the man by the coffeemaker turning around, two of the men around the table rising to their feet. Firing simultaneously with his dart launcher and the silenced Colt, Steele dropped the two in front of the TV and the one by the refrigerator. A quick shift of aim with his left arm and the one by the coffeemaker fell, all before any of the guards had time to react to his presence in their midst. And then their reaction time caught up to him.

"*Jesus*! What the *hell* . . . ?"

"*Look out!*"

"*Son of a bitch!*"

Steele brought the Colt around and shot the two men who had risen from their chairs. Two of the others at the table were rising and reaching for their sidearms. The Colt coughed twice more and they were hurled back over their chairs, a bullet through the center of each of their foreheads. The fifth man had thrown himself out of his chair and was rushing for the door leading to the hallway. Just as he reached it, Steele dropped him with a shot through the base of his spine. He heard footsteps quickly running up the stairs to the side entrance from the yard and spun around. The Colt fired twice and dropped two guards as they came running through the door, leaving the pistol empty. Steele tucked it in his waistband and ran through the door into the darkened hallway.

Twenty seconds had elapsed.

He switched from thermal imagining to night vision as he ran down the hallway, looking for the door leading to the basement stairs. According to Raven, it was on his left, about fifteen to twenty feet down the hall. He could hear someone shouting from somewhere in the house.

"What the hell happened to the power?"

He reached the door without encountering anyone in the hallway and wrenched it open.

"Relax," someone responded. "The generator'll kick in in a minute. They probably blew a fuse or something down at the plant."

"I can't see a goddamn thing!"

Steele hurried down the stairs.

Twenty-five seconds.

He made it to the basement and quickly looked around. Raven had never been down here, and she didn't know exactly where the auxiliary generators were. It was a large basement, unfinished and mostly open. Numerous storage crates were piled up all around. Steele spotted the huge boiler and the water heaters. Where the hell were the generators?

Thirty seconds.

He ran to the wall beneath the guard lounge, where the power lines from the junction box outside should have been routed. He had to thread his way through piles of crates to get there. He had no idea what was in them. Arms, perhaps, or drugs. Maybe even stored food. The Borodinis were into everything.

Thirty-five seconds.

He could hear running footsteps on the floor above him.
They'd either discovered the dead guards already or would in
seconds.

Forty seconds. . . .

There they were! He ran over to them and bent down to
start disabling the motors.

Fifty seconds. . . .

One was out. Now for the other.

Fifty-three. . . .

Come on, come on. . . .

Fifty-seven. . . .

Got it!

From upstairs, he heard a shout, sounding muffled through
the floor.

"Christ! We've been hit!"

"Higgins!" Steele said. "I've cut the power! Go!"

"Okay, we're coming in. Get Borodini!"

"Holy shit! Where the hell's the power? What happened to
the fucking generators?"

"We've got intruders! Sound the alarm!"

"*What* alarm? The fuckin' power's out!"

"They must've got the generators!"

"Someone's in the basement!"

"Come on! Move! *Move!*"

Steele heard footsteps coming down the stairs.

Sharp was driving at top speed down the Long Island
Expressway, punishing the suspension as the armored unit
hurtled over the cracked and buckled roadway. Weeds grew
through fissures in the highway. The road was totally deserted. There was not a sign of life. He passed Lake Success,
just across the border from Queens in Nassau County. County
lines had long since ceased to mean anything except as refer-
ences for geographic location. There was no government out
here except for that provided by the enclaves. The towns and
villages were mostly deserted, falling into ruin, with only
outlaws, derelicts and screamers struggling for survival in
total desolation. The surviving residents had long since gone
to the enclaves for protection. Most of Long Island was a

vast, deserted no-man's-land, slowly reverting to wilderness. And Sharp was on his own, heading at top speed straight into an ambush that waited for him at the coliseum.

He was now less than two miles from the turnoff for the Meadowbrook Parkway, which ran south all the way down to Jones Beach. Once he made the turnoff for the parkway, it was only a few miles to the Nassau Coliseum, located just outside the deserted town of Hempstead. Once a sports arena, in the years immediately following the Bio-War, stories had it that the coliseum had been used as an arena for much more savage games staged by outlaw gangs that roamed the Island, preying on survivors until the enclaves had been formed. Sharp had no idea what, if anything, it was used for now. But he was certain of at least one thing. Today, it would be used as a killing ground.

Lookouts posted on the nearby abandoned dormitory towers of what had once been Hofstra University would be able to see for miles in all directions and give warning in plenty of time if any backup units started coming in by ground or chopper. Sharp knew that if he reached the coliseum and went in there before the enclave could be secured and Borodini captured, chances were he would not come out again. He was speeding to his death, and there was nothing he could do about it.

He took the turnoff for the parkway and started heading south. His heart raced. He felt sweat running down his back as the vehicle careened down the deserted parkway.

"HQ to Bagman; HQ to Bagman, come in."

Sharp grabbed for the handset.

"Bagman here; go ahead, HQ."

"The fox is in the henhouse. Repeat, the fox is in the henhouse. Proceed as directed and stand by."

"Roger, HQ. Bagman out."

Steele was inside, and the assault was in progress! Sharp felt adrenalin hammer through his system.

"Go, Steele," he said, through gritted teeth. "Go, go, *go*!"

Steele quickly released the lock on his turret attachment,

popped it off and reattached it to his belt. He bent his elbow
back and rammed the stump of his wrist into the polymer/
ceramic, 4.7 mm. machine pistol attachment on his belt and
twisted it free as it locked into place on his left wrist. It gave
his left forearm the appearance of having a flat black two-by-
four, slightly over a foot long, sprouting from his wrist.

The trigger mechanism, safety, and select fire systems
were all internal, slaved to his cybernetic brain the moment
the pistol attachment was in place. The select fire system
gave him the options of semiautomatic, three-round burst or
full auto. A fifty-round magazine was snapped in place along
the top of the barrel, with a second barrel offset underneath
the first, aligned with the dart launcher built into his left
forearm.

The bullets in the magazine were fed into the chamber by
means of a gas-operated, cylindrical bolt that rotated ninety
degrees to align the cartridge with the barrel, a system that
was simple and highly reliable. With no rearward bolt travel,
the cycling system was extremely brief, allowing a high rate
of fire, up to 2,000 rounds per minute. The caseless ammunition was only a fraction of the size of a conventional cartridge, square in cross-section, reducing friction in the magazine
and affording maximum use of space. The fully combustible
cartridge meant that there was no brass to be ejected, and the
projectile was propelled at 3,000 feet per second. Polymer/
ceramic construction eliminated the need for maintenance and
cleaning, as well as doing away with overheating. It was a
scaled-down version of the Strike Force battle rifle, designed
to function as a part of him, completely thought-controlled. It
could not jam, and slaved to his computer brain, it could not
miss.

It didn't.

He opened up with three-round bursts as the men reached
the foot of the stairs. The rate of fire was so quick that a
three-round burst sounded like one shot. He fired four quick
bursts, and the corpses tumbled to the floor. By then, he was
already moving, having the advantage of being able to see
clearly in the dark. Two of the men in front had been carrying
flashlights. One broke when they fell, the other hit the floor

and rolled, its beam illuminating the bottoms of several crates. The men behind them on the stairs caught a brief glimpse of something moving toward them quickly, something with two red eyes that glowed like lasers in the dark, and then the machine pistol cracked out several bursts, and their bodies rolled to the bottom of the stairs.

Steele swept up one of their .308 assault rifles as he rushed up the stairs, leaping over the bodies. Several men carrying weapons came running down the hall from both sides, some of the guards coming from inside the mansion, others rushing in from the outside. There was a lot of shouting. Steele fired to his left and right simultaneously, several bursts from his machine pistol, an extended burst on full auto from the rifle, firing it one-handed and emptying the magazine. Their bodies dropped, piling into one another as the spent brass from the .308 pattered to the floor like hot metal raindrops.

He dropped the empty rifle, ran to his left, down the hall leading into the mansion, bending down over one of the bodies as he passed and retrieving its assault rifle. As he reached the end of the hall, he heard growling and the patter of paws on the floor behind him. He spun around as two dogs came hurtling down the hallway toward him. He dropped one in mid-leap with a dart and brought up his right arm, still holding the rifle, as the second dog struck him and fastened onto his nysteel forearm. He pressed the pistol up against the dog's underbelly and fired a dart into it. The animal gave a brief whimper and dropped to the floor like a sack.

Steele turned and ran through the darkened east wing of the mansion, into its spacious entry hall. The large, wide flight of stairs leading to the second floor was to his right, the front entrance to his left. The stairway went halfway up to the second floor, then split off at the landing into two separate flights of stairs, leading up to the left and right. The front door flew open and several armed men came running in. Steele fired three short bursts with his machine pistol and dropped them in their tracks. Beyond them, through the front door, he could see three dogs running at full speed across the lawn. As they came flying up the front steps, he reached the front door, slammed it shut and threw the bolt. An automatic

weapon opened up behind him, and bullets peppered the front
door beside him. He felt several of them impacting on his
back. He raised the assault rifle and fired it one-handed. The
gunman on the stairs dropped his weapon and rolled down to
the landing. Steele took the stairs three at a time.

Sharp was doing well over a hundred as he hit the turnoff
for the coliseum. According to his watch, he had only minutes before his allotted time ran out, both figuratively and
literally. He glanced down at the radio, willing it to come to
life and speak to him. Come on, Steele, he thought. Come
on, dammit! If he didn't have Victor Borodini for a bargain-
ing chip by the time he got there, he'd be on his own against
Tommy B and his soldiers. And he didn't think much of his
chances.

The choppers came in low over Centre Island, crossing
Oyster Bay Harbor, across the spit of land separating Oyster
Bay from Cold Spring Harbor. The jet-powered X-wing with
Ice and Raven in it was in the vanguard, well ahead of all the
others.

"Come on, man! Can't you make this crate go any faster?"
Raven shouted to the pilot.

"Keep your shirt on, miss," the pilot said through his
helmet speaker. "We'll be there in less than thirty seconds."

"A man can die in less than thirty seconds!" she responded.

"Then if you want to help him, you'll shut up," said the
pilot. "I'm going to have my hands full. Target's within
range."

He came sweeping in low over the grounds in a wide arc,
flying over the village and banking around to line up on the
sentry towers on the wall surrounding it. The muzzle flash of
automatic weapons fire erupted from two of the towers as he
came in toward them and fired two rockets. Both hit dead on
target, and the towers exploded in twin fireballs as he hurtled
through the wash of flame, angling the nose down and sweeping the grounds with his machinegun turrets. Mines exploded
as bullets struck, and bodies flew into the air. As the guards
below scattered, several of them panicked and ran into the

minefields, tripping the detonators and blowing themselves up.

"All *right*!" said Ice, grinning from ear to ear. "This *my* kind of party!"

Suddenly, the floodlights on the grounds came back on.

"What the *hell*?" the pilot said. "I thought Steele took out the generators!"

The chopper slowed, flying on rotor power now as they passed over the mansion's roof and saw men running out to the shore batteries covering the harbor, swinging them around and elevating the guns. The pilot fired a rocket and one of the batteries went up in an explosion of flame. The men operating the other battery were desperately bringing it around and elevating it towards the chopper when he fired another rocket, and the gun emplacement went up in a ball of fire. All the lights were on inside the mansion. The surface-to-air missile batteries rose up from the lawn.

"*Jesus Christ*," the pilot said. "They're gonna fly right into it!"

Even as he spoke, a couple of missiles left the launchers, hurtling toward the incoming choppers. The pilot fired another rocket, taking out one of the batteries, then swung around to bring his aim to bear on another one.

"Get us *down* there!" Raven shouted.

"I can't!" the pilot said. "I've got to knock out those missiles!"

"There's too many of them!" Raven shouted. "You'll never get them all in time!"

"I've gotta try!"

Two more missiles left their launchers. The pilot fired again.

"Get us down there, dammit!" Raven shouted.

"Back off!"

Ice pressed the barrel of his battle rifle up against the back of the pilot's helmet.

"Lady said to get us down there," he said. "*Now*."

"Don't be a damn fool! You shoot me and we all die!"

"I don't gotta kill you, whitebread," Ice said, moving around and shifting the barrel of the gun. He pressed it down into the pilot's groin. "You ever consider bein' Jewish?"

"You're fuckin' crazy!"

"You got that right. Just set us down. The roof do fine."

"All right, all right!"

He hovered low over the rooftop and Raven leaped down out of the hatch.

"Thank'ee kindly," Ice said with a grin, then turned and dropped down after her.

"Crazy son of a bitch!" the pilot said. And as he raised up over the roof, he saw the first of the surface-to-air missiles strike the incoming choppers.

As the lights came on all over the mansion, Steele froze at the top of the stairs.

"Fuck!"

There could be only one explanation. Something Raven hadn't told him. Something Raven hadn't known. The control room had its own auxiliary generator. Victor Borodini's paranoia had served him well. Borodini's quarters were down the hall, to his left. The control room was at the far end of the hallway to his right. There was no time for Borodini now. The choppers would be coming in, heading right into a swarm of surface-to-air missiles.

Steele sprinted down the hallway to his right. Someone fired at him from one of the rooms halfway down the hall. Steele didn't even pause. He kept right on running at full speed as the bullets whistled past him and slammed into his chest and shoulder. Steele fired the assault rifle, stitching the wall as he ran past the gunman, bullets tracking their way across the doorway and ploughing through his chest. As the man fell back into the room behind him, Steele didn't pause. His legs churned as he raced toward the door of the control room at the far end of the hall and slammed into it full speed, bursting the steel-reinforced door off its hinges.

The three men at the control panels looked up in shock as he opened up with both his machine pistol and the assault rifle on full auto, spraying the entire control room. The bodies of the three men sprayed blood and jerked like marionettes as the bullets struck them and smashed into the control panels and the radar monitors, sending out showers of sparks.

Smoke billowed out from the control panels, flames licked up from the consoles. Steele kept firing till both weapons were empty, then he dropped the rifle to the floor, twisted the empty magazine out of his machine pistol and snapped in a fresh one from his belt. The lights flickered, but stayed on. The generator was still supplying power, but the control panels smoked and sputtered, burning and shooting out sparks. The defense systems were now useless. The surface-to-air missile batteries had been disabled. Steele heard the crackle of a battle rifle behind him in the hall and spun around in time to see a gunman fall behind him. A moment later, Raven came down the stairs from the roof with Ice right behind her. He hurried to meet them.

"Sweep across on full auto, right?" said Raven with a grin.

"Right," said Steele.

They heard the staccato beat of helicopter blades outside and above them, and there was the sound of automatic weapons fire as the assault units disembarked and engaged the remaining enclave security personnel on the ground.

"Where's Borodini?" Ice said.

"I don't know," said Steele. "Down that way somewhere, I guess."

They ran down the hall toward Borodini's quarters, Ice covering their backs. Steele reached the door and kicked it in. There was no one in the main room of the suite, but Steele's amplified hearing picked up the sounds of breathing in the room beyond. Two people.

"In there," he said.

"The bedroom," Raven said.

"Stand back," said Ice.

He fired a burst at the lock and kicked open the door.

Paulie Borodini sat up in the large canopied bed, eyes wide, naked and holding the covers up against him, his long black hair cascading over his slender, pale shoulders. His father stood beside the bed, wearing nothing but a black silk dressing gown, bordered in gold and embroidered with his monogram over his breast. He held a black semiautomatic in his right hand.

"Steele," he said in an emotionless tone. "I might have known."

Raven caught her breath as she looked from Paulie to Borodini with disbelief. "*Paulie*? My God, Victor. . . ." she said. Then words simply failed her.

The corner of Victor Borodini's mouth twitched slightly. "Ravenna," he said. "What a surprise. I'd often wondered what became of you. And Ice, too. I knew I should have killed you from the start. Careless of me."

"Drop the gun, Borodini," Steele said.

"I don't think so," Borodini said. "It's all over anyway, isn't it? And you've exposed my guilty secret. You may as well finish the job." He glanced toward the slender, long-haired boy sitting up in the bed. "Dear Paulie," he said. "So like his mother . . ."

"Put the gun down, Borodini," Steele said. "I'm not going to kill you. I need you alive."

Borodini glanced at him with a bemused expression. "Do you, indeed? Well, in that case, it will give me great pleasure to disappoint you."

He raised the gun to his head, but before he could pull the trigger, Steele's lightning reflexes switched the machine pistol to semiautomatic mode and fired. The bullet struck the gun and sent it flying. Borodini gasped with pain and clutched his wrist, wincing. He looked up at Steele with venom in his eyes.

"Damn you to hell!" he said through gritted teeth.

"Higgins," Steele said. "Get hold of Sharp. Mission accomplished. The enclave is secured. We've got Victor Borodini."

"Good work, Steele. I'm calling Sharp right now. Stand by."

Paulie slowly shook his head. "I don't understand," he said softly. "It was a good plan. A good plan. What could have gone wrong?"

Sharp was out of time. He slowed as he approached the coliseum and saw the service bays open, waiting to admit him. No word from Higgins. Damn it, he thought. He swallowed hard. There was nothing for it. He had to play for time. He'd have to go in and hope like hell he could bluff his way through. What could they have in there that could take out an armored Strike Force unit? Plenty, he thought. Rocket launchers would do the trick just fine. If he didn't get out with the money, they could fry him where he sat. Or riddle the unit with armor-piercing ammo until it looked like a Swiss cheese and then simply come in and pick up the money. It might have a few holes shot through it and some of it might be a little bloody, but what the hell.

He slowly drove the unit through the service bay and on through into the arena. Maybe I can bluff them, he thought. Maybe I can buy some time—

The radio came to life. *"HQ to Bagman. HQ to Bagman. Enclave is secured. Repeat, enclave is secured. We've got Borodini. Acknowledge."*

Sharp almost sobbed with relief. "Roger, HQ. I'm at the rendezvous. About to make contact. I'm going to need some proof to convince them. And I'm gonna need it in a hurry."

"You'll have it. Stand by. We'll patch through to the enclave."

Then Sharp heard Tommy B's voice from somewhere up in the seats above him.

"Okay, Steele. End of the line. It's payoff time! Get out of the car and bring the money."

"Okay, Sharp, we're patching you through. Stand by."

Sharp switched on his PA. He took off his helmet and spoke without the synthesizer disguising his voice.

"It isn't Steele, Tommy," he said, his amplified voice echoing throughout the arena. "Steele's at the enclave. It's been captured. Our agents have secured it. And we've got your father."

There was a brief silence.

"What *is* this?" Tommy shouted. "Who the hell are *you*? And where the fuck is Steele?"

"My name is Sharp. Central Intelligence. It's over, Tommy," Sharp said into the mike. "While you were running me all over thinking I was Steele, Steele attacked the enclave with an assault unit and captured it. We have your father in custody. We'll make you a swap. Your old man for the hostages.''

"You think I'm some kind of idiot?'' Tommy shouted. "You expect me to fall for that shit? You're *dead*, you motherfucker. The fucking hostages are dead, you *hear* me?''

"You don't have to take my word for it, Tommy,'' Sharp said quickly. "We're patching your father through. Listen for yourself.''

Steele took the radio one of the agents had given him and held it up to Borodini. "Talk to your son,'' he said.

Borodini smiled and shook his head.

"Do like the man say, Victor,'' Ice said, "or I start havin' target practice with little Paulie here.''

Borodini stared at him. "You're bluffing,'' he said.

Ice shot Paulie in the shoulder.

Paulie cried out and fell back on the bed, clutching at his shoulder. Blood spread out, staining the sheets.

"All right! All right!'' cried Borodini, panic-stricken. "My God, don't! I'll do anything you say!''

"Talk,'' said Ice.

Steele held up the radio.

Borodini's voice, patched in through Sharp's radio, came out over the unit's PA.

"Tommy? Tommy, it's your father. Do what they say. They've taken the enclave. I'm their prisoner. Do whatever they tell you.''

Tommy glanced at Rick. "It's gotta be a trick,'' he said. "I don't believe it. They could never take the enclave. Never.''

"It's Papa's voice,'' said Rick.

"Yeah, and it was Steele's voice I heard over the phone, only it wasn't Steele,'' Tommy said. "It's a trick, I tell you!''

"How do we know for sure?''

Tommy yelled down to the arena. "I ain't fallin' for it, Sharp,'' he said. "It's a trick! You already tried that once with Steele's voice, and I ain't fallin' for it again! You hear me? You got ten seconds to get out of that car with the money, asshole! Ten seconds! And if you brought the money,

I just *might* let you live. If you're lucky. Otherwise, I'll blow you to fuckin' smithereens!''

"He doesn't believe it," Sharp said tensely. "He thinks it's another trick, like with the synthesizer. Come up with something fast, I'm in a lot of trouble here!"

"He doesn't believe it's you," said Steele. "Say something only you and he would know."

"Better make it good," said Ice, "or Paulie be hurtin'."

"You people are barbarians!" said Borodini.

Steele stared at him and held up the radio. "You said it yourself, Borodini. I'm not even human. I'm just a machine, right?" He smiled grimly. "No feelings. A robot. Nothing but cold steel."

Borodini swallowed hard and moistened his lips. "Tommy," he said, "Tommy, listen to me. . . ."

". . . remember what I told you when Caravelli blew the hit on Steele?" Borodini's voice came over the radio and through the vehicle's PA. *"Remember how I called you to my room and said you disappointed me? Remember how I was upset about the warrants, and you didn't understand because you thought we were too strong for that to bother us? I told you that there's a lot more to running the family than simply being strong. You have to be smart as well. You have to know how to figure the odds and play the percentages. I told you that we had to think about the future. You remember, Tommy?"*

Rick Borodini watched his brother's face as the realization dawned on him that Sharp was telling them the truth.

"It's him," Rick said. "It's not a trick. It's Papa. That's what he always used to say."

"Shut up!" snapped Tommy.

"We have to think about the future now, Tommy," Victor Borodini continued. *"We have to think about the family. About you and Rick and Paulie."* Borodini glanced at his wounded son, pain written all over his face. *"We've lost for now, but we can build it all again. We can put it back together if we play it smart. And next time, we'll be ready for them. They've won this time, but it's not over. We'll come*

back stronger, and next time, they won't stop us. Not the feds, not the Delanos, not the Pastoris or the Castellanos, nobody! But we gotta play it smart, Tommy. We gotta know when to fold the cards. Do what they tell you, Tommy. This isn't a defeat. It's just a setback.''

"That's it," said Rick. "They've got us by the shorthairs. We're going to have to cut a deal."

"No!" said Tommy, turning on him angrily. "Fuck, no! No deals! We've got the hostages! They do what *we* tell 'em! They do what *I* say! They play it *my* way or I start sending 'em bodies!"

"And they start sending us pieces of Papa and Paulie in plastic bags," said Rick. "Don't think they won't. These people ain't the cops, they're feds. CIA. They don't have to answer to the city administration or public opinion. It's a standoff. We've got the hostages, they've got Papa and Paulie. And we can't put things back together without them or the rest of our people. We'll cut a deal, straight across. We release half the hostages, they give us Papa and half the prisoners they took. We release the other half, they give up Paulie and the others."

"No!" shouted Tommy. *"No way!* I ain't doin' it! I ain't givin' in to those bastards!"

"We have no choice," said Rick calmly. "With the enclave gone, we've got a lousy hand. It's like Papa said, Tommy, you have to know when to fold the cards."

"Forget it!" Tommy shouted, his eyes wild. "So they got the enclave. So they got the old man and Paulie. *So fuckin' what?* We got our people in the city! We still got the gangs, we still got our soldiers! We got our warehouses and our connections!"

"What are you talking about?" said Rick. "Calm down, for Christ's sake. Without Paulie, we can't put the business back together and you know it. Without Papa, we lose all our people, our soldiers, our connections, everything. You're talking crazy. Who's gonna run things, you?"

"Yeah, *me*! Why the hell not? You think I can't do it?"

"And what about our people at the enclave? What about Papa and Paulie?"

"Fuck 'em! Who the hell needs 'em? What's the old man ever done for me but run me down? What's he ever done for you but give you orders like you're some kinda flunky? And as for Paulie, he's just a fuckin' wimp. He's useless. He's a zero! They want me to call their bluff? All right, I'm fuckin' *callin'* it! I'm gonna waste *all* the goddamn hostages, Sanderson and all the rest of 'em, every fuckin' one! And I'm startin' right now with that son of a bitch down there, that bastard!"

"No, you're not."

"Get outta my way! *I'm* in charge now! I'm gonna ice that son of a bitch right *now*!"

"Tommy, don't. . . ."

Tommy snatched up the rocket launcher.

"Tommy!"

"Hey, Sharp!" screamed Tommy. "Kiss it goodbye, you son of a bitch!"

A single shot cracked out, its echo reverberating throughout the coliseum.

"Hold your fire!" Rick shouted to their men stationed in the stands around the arena.

"Sharp?" said Steele, over the radio. *"What's happening?"*

Sharp sat perfectly still, holding his breath and waiting for the flaming end, every single muscle in his body tense.

"Mr. Sharp? Can you hear me?"

Sharp picked up the mike. His hand was shaking.

"I hear you."

"This is Rick Borodini, Mr. Sharp. My brother and I have had a little disagreement. I'm afraid he's not going to be party to our negotiation. You can come out of the car now. No one's going to shoot. I'm coming down to meet you. Tell Steele that we can do some business."

11

"All in all, I'm quite pleased with the way everything turned out," said Higgins. "We had to give up Victor Borodini and the rest of the prisoners we took, but the hostages were all released unharmed. We've broken the Borodinis' hold on the gangs in no-man's-land, driven them out of their enclave and left them without a power base, at the mercy of the other crime families. And they'll be so busy competing with each other to see who gets to pick up Borodini's action that it'll be quite a while before they can cause us any serious trouble. On top of that, we've established a foothold in Long Island now that we've got their enclave, a positive first step toward re-establishing some law and order out there. And it only cost us three helicopters, three pilots and about a dozen agents."

"Was that all?" said Steele.

"It could have been much worse," said Higgins, ignoring his sarcasm. "You've proved yourself yet again, sustaining only some minor damage in the process, and the publicity we got from rescuing the hostages and breaking the Borodini family was pure gold. My superiors are very pleased. With both of us."

"Swell," said Steele dryly.

"You don't sound very happy about it," Higgins said. "What's wrong?"

"Victor Borodini walked," said Steele. "That's what's wrong."

"Yes, well, under the circumstances, I think we came out well ahead. And at least we won't have Tommy B to worry about anymore. Killed by his own brother. Boy, that's some family.''

"Yeah," said Steele. "And we had to 'do business' with them, as Rick put it." He snorted with derision. "*Business.* They run hookers, protection rackets, drugs and arms, muscle in on half the action in no-man's-land, take hostages and kill people and they get to walk. All except for Tommy, and Rick took care of him, purely as a matter of self-interest. It turned my stomach to have to negotiate with him."

Higgins shrugged. "Sooner or later, Steele, everybody does business with everybody. You might as well get used to it. It's what makes the world go round."

"Your world, maybe," Steele said. "Not mine. But while we're on the subject, what about Ice? He played it straight with us and he was a big help. You promised him immunity. I hope you intend to live up to your agreement."

"Absolutely," Higgins said. "In fact, I've done better than that. I could use a man of his abilities. I made the offer, and he's already accepted. I believe his exact words were, 'Ain't got nuthin' else to do.' All he wanted to know was if the apartment came with the job. And he said he would prefer to work with you. I hope you don't have any objections. He makes most of my other people a bit nervous."

Steele smiled faintly. "No, I don't have any objections."

"Good," said Higgins. "By the way, there's someone waiting outside to see you. I promised to call her as soon as you were out of surgery. Dr. Cooper seemed very anxious to speak with you, but he's not in right now, and I figure it can wait. Take a few days off and relax. You've earned it."

"Thanks," said Steele.

He got up and left the office. Higgins reached for his phone and punched in the extension of the project chief of security.

"Connors?" he said. "This is Higgins. You've still got your tail on Dr. Cooper, I trust?"

"Yes, sir. You gave me no orders to the contrary."

"Good. Where is he right now?"

"My man just checked in a few minutes ago," said Connors. "He's at St. Vincent's on 66th. and Lex. He apparently went to confession. But according to his file, he's not a Roman Catholic."

Higgins smiled. "No, he's not," he said. "He went to have a talk with Father Liam Casey. Something very metaphysical, no doubt, about the nature of the human soul."

"Sir?"

"Never mind," said Higgins. "I want you to send one of your people over to Dr. Cooper's apartment on Sutton Place. Right now. Someone who knows his way around computers. I'll set up a secure phone line for a download. I think I'd like to have a closer look at what he's been doing with that backup program."

"Right away, sir."

Higgins hung up and leaned back in his chair, his arms folded across his chest. He frowned. What are you up to, Cooper? he thought. What the devil are you up to?

Raven was waiting for him outside in the reception area, sitting with her legs crossed, reading a magazine and smoking a cigarette. The marine guards were all standing at their posts, but they couldn't take their eyes off her. She wore a very short black leather skirt that showed her long and shapely legs to excellent advantage. She had on black suede boots with high spike heels and a black leather vest, held together by two buttons, with absolutely nothing underneath it. She looked up as he came out.

"Hi," he said.

"Hi," she replied, a bit uncertainly, stubbing out her cigarette and getting to her feet. "I . . . I just wanted to make sure you were okay. You know, with everything that was going on, I didn't realize you'd been shot. I mean . . . there wasn't any blood on you or anything, and I didn't even know about it until I found out you'd gone in for surgery."

"More like a short trip to the body shop," said Steele with a wry grin. "It was only minor damage, mostly cosmetic. They dug out some bullets, replaced some polymer skin, tightened a few nuts and bolts, no big deal."

"Well . . . I . . . I just wanted to make sure you were okay," she said. She hesitated slightly. "I can have my stuff out of your apartment by tonight. Maybe tomorrow at the latest. I mean, if that's okay.''

He stared at her. ''You're leaving?''

She looked down, avoiding his gaze, and moistened her lips nervously. ''Well . . . now that it's all over, I . . . I wasn't sure if you wanted me to stay.''

Steele reached out and lifted her chin gently, bringing her face up so that he could look into her large dark eyes.

''Stay,'' he said.

HIGH-TECH, HARD-EDGED ACTION!
All-new series!

__**STEELE** J.D. Masters 1-55773-219-1/$3.50
Lt. Donovan Steele—one of the best cops around, until he was killed. Now he's been rebuilt--the perfect combination of man and machine, armed with the firepower of a high-tech army!

__**FREEDOM'S RANGERS** Keith William Andrews 0-425-11643-3/$3.95
An elite force of commandos fights the battles of the past to save America's future—this time it's 1923 and the Rangers are heading to Berlin to overthrow Adolf Hitler! Look for Book Two—*Raiders of the Revolution*--coming in November!

__**TANKWAR** Larry Steelbaugh 0-425-11741-3/$3.50
On the battlefields of World War III, Sergeant Max Tag and his crew take on the Soviet army with the most sophisticated high-tech tank ever built. On sale in November.

__**SPRINGBLADE** Greg Walker 1-55773-266-3/$2.95
Bo Thornton—Vietnam vet, Special Forces, Green Beret. Now retired, he's leading a techno-commando team—men who'll take on the dirtiest fighting jobs and won't leave until justice is done.

__**THE MARAUDERS** Michael McGann 0-515-10150-8/$2.95
World War III is over, but enemy forces are massing in Europe, plotting the ultimate takeover. And the Marauders—guerrilla freedom fighters—aren't waiting around for the attack. They're going over to face it head-on!

LOOK FOR THE NEW SERIES—
COMMAND AND CONTROL—BY JAMES D. MITCHELL
COMING IN DECEMBER!